KISS

FILE JC 110

Other titles by the same author

Your Friend, Rebecca

The Damned

Nightmare Park

Emmeline Pankhurst (biography)

Poems for Peace (ed.)

The Alternative Assembly Book (with Mike Hoy)

KISS
FILE JC 110

LINDA HOY

WALKER BOOKS
LONDON

First published 1988 by Walker Books Ltd
87 Vauxhall Walk, London SE11 5HJ

First printed 1988
Printed in Great Britain by Billings & Sons Ltd, Worcester
Typest by Graphicraft Typesetters Ltd, Hong Kong

British Library Cataloguing in Publication Data
Hoy, Linda
Kiss File JC 110.
I. Title
823'.914[F] PZ7
ISBN 0-7445-0826-6

"Yet each man kills the thing he loves,
By each let this be heard,
Some do it with a bitter look,
Some with a flattering word,
The coward does it with a kiss,
The brave man with a sword!"

The Ballad of Reading Gaol
Oscar Wilde

"And the Government shall be upon his shoulder"

Isaiah 9:6

Inside the foyer I wait for the lift. I smile across at the doorman and hum a tune to myself as I watch the numbers glow: 8 . . . 7 . . . 6 . . . 5 . . . 4 . . . 5 . . . 6 . . . Shit. I start to pull at my earlobe and then stop myself. It's a silly, nervous habit I've had since I was a kid – pulling at my earlobes when I'm angry. I tap my foot instead.

The other lift arrives. It's empty. I walk inside and press floor 8. While I'm on my own, I look myself up and down: trousers OK; flies done up; jacket sleeves nice and straight. I start to pick my nose and then remember that I don't want to dirty my handkerchief, ironed and folded like a neat little sandwich. I want to look smart. I force myself to wait patiently, my arms down by my sides. A soldier standing to attention.

I remember how nervous I was the first time I was here. I thought they'd be watching me. Cameras everywhere. I daren't pick my nose in the lift. I thought they'd have it on video, watching me and laughing. Then I had this obsession that I might have trodden in some dog dirt. I could imagine it ponging out the interview room. I remembered hopping out of the lift, craning my neck to check out the undersides of my shoes and then colliding with the tea trolley.

The lift stops and I walk out into the corridor.

Now I know they do have cameras. Watching you. All over the place. I've seen the videotapes myself. You never know where the electronic eyes are, scrutinizing every move. But now it doesn't matter. I accept it as part of the job. They must have film of me walking down the street, standing in the lift and doing all kinds of private things I'd much rather do on my own. But surveillance is part of the job. I understand that now. I don't let it bother me any more.

"Good morning."

I've not seen this Boss before – a thin man with his suit hanging off him in folds. The office looks the same: tired wallpaper, frosted glass like the windows of a public lavatory and a pot of decaying plants which look like overgrown dock leaves. "Good morning, Sir." I shake his hand firmly. Everything tells in this job.

"Have a seat."

"Thank you."

I pull a chair up to the desk, sit down and wait patiently while he searches for the file and papers I expected him to have ready. He ought to have them ready, on the money they pay him for sitting here, playing at spies. I try to look eager, ready for anything. In school they always chose me to be monitor: milk monitor, library monitor, homework monitor – the one who told the teachers who'd been copying their homework in the bog.

"A new assignment." The Boss has finally found a tattered old manila folder, held together with Sellotape. There are stock rooms of new folders in this place. Their meanness is unbelievable.

I nod at him.

He swings the folder in between his bony fingers. "This man . . . " he nods at the folder, "is a threat to national security." He utters the words carefully and slowly.

Not another nutcase. I try to look impressed.

"He has a certain . . . what do you call it? A personality . . . a persona."

All the personality of a soggy cornflake I should imagine. They're always trying to make out that these characters are exciting. Undersized, underprivileged, underestimated James Bonds. And they work with all the frenetic enthusiasm of old-aged pensioners nicking tubes of Steradent from the Co-op. We've never had a proper car chase yet. These characters ride bikes. Or go on the bus. Double-crossing them is like high-jacking a three-year-old on his way home from the nursery school. If you sent Frankenstein's monster along in a pink-flowered bonnet they'd mistake him for their grandmother.

The Boss looks at me. I'm supposed to ask intelligent

questions. That's what this is all about: intelligence. I look at the thickness of the folder. "Somebody's been working on this already . . . ?"

He nods. "For the last three years. Other members of the family have also been under surveillance. The subject's mother is a known Trotskyist, an associate of Militant Tendency. The father has been known to give financial sponsorship to subversive organizations."

He pats the folder. "We have transcripts of telephone conversations . . . letters . . . the transcripts are in here." He hands me the folder. I lay it on my knee. I'll look at it later on. I need to hype myself up for two hours of total boredom. The telephone directory would make a more exciting read. I start to rise.

The interview isn't over. "Grow your hair a bit longer," he tells me.

Why the hell can't I have my hair the way I like it? I sigh. "Yes, Sir."

"Can you grow a beard?"

I can't stand beards. I'd look like a prehistoric hippy. Who on earth does he think I am? I pull gently on my earlobe yet again. "All right," I tell him. "I'll grow a beard."

"Maybe a moustache as well. It'll hide that scar on your lip."

I got that scar on the last job. Not in a car chase or wrestling with man-eating sharks. I got it falling off a ladder. I was pretending to be a window cleaner while peering through these windows for nearly an hour in the middle of January. Trundling up and down the ladder and wiping the glass with my frozen washleather. In the end my fingers got so numb I fell off the blinking ladder and the bucket hit me in the mouth. And the ice-cold water fell over my head.

"Yes, I'll try a moustache, Sir," I tell him. Now we are playing at spies. I wish he'd grow up. They all see themselves as little generals moving us round on a board – none of us know what it's for or who it is that's in charge. We're never told who we're really after, what they've done or why they've done it. We're just doing our job. We don't know any of the answers. They call it security. They think we're a load of mugs.

He stands up. "I'll expect a report from you every four weeks," he tells me. "Hand delivered."

"Yes, Sir."

I don't shake his hand so firmly as I leave.

I prepare myself for an evening of absolute monotony with a couple of cans of lager and a carton of frozen mince pies. When I get to be James Bond, I'll drink whisky and eat my meals in restaurants.

I put the mince pies under the grill. While I'm waiting for them to defrost I open up the folder.

The first part is an exercise book – a young kid's exercise book that looks as if his father has brought it home from work for him. I lean back and sigh in disgust. What do they take me for? Intelligence files on school kids? Who do they think I am? A child minder? I yank the top off my lager and sling the ring over to the plastic willow-pattern bin. I applied for this job because I thought it would be exciting. If I'd wanted to sit and watch kiddies all day long I'd have tried to get a job as a teacher. Or a lollipop man.

I smell the mince pies burning. I fish them out and start to scrape off their tops. Warm mince pies make me think of Christmas – of families and firesides. It spoils them, not having lids. I put them on a tray, go back in front of the gas fire, open the file and try again.

I glance through and see that the first part of the file is papers and stuff from three years ago; the back of the file is up to date. I do a few sums and work out that means they've been keeping tabs on this kid since he was – it takes me a while to work it out – since he was nearly fifteen years old.

I take a long swig at the lager and then I start to read.

* * *

Ministry of Defence
Main Building
Whitehall
LONDON SW1A 2H8

"D" Notices on British Intelligence Services
and Ciphers and Communications

PRIVATE AND CONFIDENTIAL

File JC 110
Part I

RIVELIN VALLEY CRIMINAL RECORDS

INPUT DATE:	05/10/81	**SEX:**	Male
SURNAME:	Christopher	**FORENAME(S):**	Julian
NICKNAME(S):	none known	**ALIAS(ES):**	none known
P.O.B:	Maidstone	**D.O.B:**	25/12/66

ADDRESS: 7 ("Highgrass"), Windermere Road, Bishopston

STREET TYPE: Upper class suburbia

ABOVE ADDRESS VERIFIED: 01/10/81

VEHICLE(S): none

HEIGHT:	4ft 10ins	**PHOTO NO:**	SB/110/3/27/84
EYE COLOUR:	blue	**BUILD:**	slim
RACE:	white	**HAIR:**	brown
FACIAL HAIR:	none	**ABNORMALITIES:**	none

RIVELIN VALLEY CRO NO: 347/84/110

SECURITY LEVEL: Special Branch

REASON(S) FOR INTEREST: Membership of subversive organizations, parents under surveillance

LAST CONVICTION DATE: no convictions

REMARKS: Membership of Young Communist League from 08/11/80
Membership of Campaign for Nuclear Disarmament (Rivelin Valley Youth Branch) from 28/01/81
Friends of the Earth membership from 18/03/70 (Family membership)

MY DIARY

KEEP OUT

PRIVATE

J Christopher

Something strange has happened. I feel I need to write it down because it seems to be important. That doesn't mean that I think I might forget about it but what I don't want to lose track of is the feeling of importance. Writing it down will help to keep it with me.

I had this friend called Rob. I was sitting on the bean bag in my bedroom with my records playing on the hi-fi when suddenly I heard a screaming in my head. That's the only way I can describe it. It was as if my brain was screaming. And for reasons I can't explain, I felt sure that it had something to do with Rob – Rob was the one who was screaming and I was hearing him in my head. I felt shaky and frightened about it – really shocked. I picked up the phone and pressed his number; the phone rang but no one answered. I calmed down then and tried to stop myself from thinking about it but the feeling was still there. It was really weird. I kept phoning his house all evening but still there was nobody there. I wanted to go round but I knew there wasn't any point. Not if there was no one in.

I phoned up later before I went to bed but still there was no answer. I went to sleep then and in the morning I didn't feel too bad. I imagined myself telling Rob about it when I got to school. I thought of how I'd say it – something funny that had happened, just something to tell him about. On the bus to school I met Chris whose dad works in the police station down the road; he told me that Rob had had an accident. He'd been knocked down on his bike the night before. It had happened when I heard him screaming in my head.

All day long I just felt shaken. To tell the truth, I wasn't all that worried about Rob. I'd been in hospital once when I'd had concussion. I'd fallen off the swings in the park when I was little. The hospital was really nice. They had teddy bears and a magic roundabout that went round and played a tune when you wound it up. They gave you ice-cream whenever you wanted and the nurses kept coming round with drinks like cola and lemonade and fizzy pop. My mum and dad only bought natural fruit juice at home so I thought it was really lovely. I didn't want to come home when I got better. That's why I didn't feel too worried about Rob.

What upset me was the screaming in my head. The screaming was something that I didn't know could happen and, when it did, there was nothing that had gone before – what my mum and dad had told me or what I'd learned at school – that could help me understand it.

In fact, because they'd told me things like that could never happen, it almost made me feel as though everything I'd learned before was wrong – a lie, even. I felt as if they'd been deceiving me. They'd always told me that all the weird and magical things you read about in books – like ghosts and spirits and telepathy – were all made up, but what I felt was that this strange and magical thing was real. It had hit me with such a shock that it seemed more real than cornflakes and teabags and eating Sunday dinner.

This wasn't actually the first strange thing that had happened. There were two others I remembered but they seemed so trivial I'd just put them down to coincidence. One was nothing really. It was just that on two occasions when I'd picked up the phone to call Rob, he'd picked the phone up at just the same second to call me. I picked up the phone to press his number and he was there already talking to me before the phone had started ringing. "That was quick," he said. What was odd was that twice that happened with Rob and never with anyone else.

The second time is more difficult to explain. We were playing Monopoly and I was the motor car and the bank. Rob had just landed on my Park Lane with two hotels and he was mortgaging everything to try and raise enough money for the rent. It was taking him ages to work out the money and I was feeling tired. I was lazing with my head on the bean bag listening to the radio and I closed my eyes a bit. I hadn't gone to sleep but sometimes, when I'm dozing like that, I get pictures floating in my head the way I do when I've gone to sleep and I'm dreaming. And the picture that floated in my head just then was of a shovel piled up high with money and then Rob said, "Shovel the money across." He wanted me to pass it him out of the bank. It seemed uncanny. "That's funny," I told him. "I was just thinking about shovels." We didn't say anything else about it. It wasn't important enough to have a conversation about. It just seemed peculiar at the time.

The next night I went to see Rob in hospital. I'd bought him a BMX magazine. I know you're supposed to take flowers and fruit and stuff to people when they're in hospital but I knew Rob wouldn't be bothered about that. He was really keen on BMX so I bought him the latest magazine. He always used to be reading them at school but usually they were somebody else's.

I could hardly believe it when I saw him. He was unconscious with a bandage wrapped around his head. There were tubes coming out all over him. One of them led to a yukky yellow plastic bag hanging near the floor. He had a plaster on the back of his hand with another tube leading to a bag on a stand by the side of his bed. There was a black mask lying on the covers near his face and that was hooked to another machine. I thought at first that he was dead. His face was greyish white and he wasn't breathing properly. He took a little breath, just a short one, and then he seemed to hold his breath for ages. When we were little we used to play at that – seeing who could hold their breath for longest – but he wasn't playing now. I thought that he was dying.

I was very shocked and my first thought was that I didn't want him to die because he'd been my closest friend for the last three years and I didn't think I could get another one. I'd have nobody to play Monopoly with. It seems really trivial and selfish when I put it like that, but that's the sort of thought that was going through my mind: who would I sit with at dinner time at school? What if I wanted to go swimming? Who would I go with?

Anyway, the nurse came and looked at the magazine and

said how Rob would read it when he got better. That reassured me. Even though I'd thought myself that he looked really ill as if he might die at any minute, she was the expert on those things: not me. I wished afterwards that she hadn't said that. My immediate feelings were that Rob was going to die and I had to get used to the idea. When the nurse said that he'd get better, I still had doubts. At school the next day I kept thinking about it – thinking about him dying, but I just tried to push the thoughts out of my mind. I wished afterwards that I hadn't – that I'd given myself more time to get used to the idea.

I went to see him again the next day after school and he was just as bad. His mum was there and a lot of other relatives gathered round the bed and I felt as if I didn't belong. When I walked inside the ward there was a different nurse on duty and she asked me if I was family. I didn't know what she meant at first and then I realized. "No," I told her. "I'm just a friend."

It seemed terrible to say *just* a friend. Because the friendship I had with Rob seemed right then to be the most important thing I had in my life. "Well, just pop in for a couple of minutes," she said.

I suppose that if I were his second cousin twice removed who hadn't seen him for the last six years, then I'd have been allowed to stay for longer. I didn't want to stay for longer anyway. As I say, I felt like an outsider. I wanted to sit with Rob on my own. I wanted to sit down next to him and tell him how much I wanted him to get better. I'd been thinking about it earlier on. I thought he might be able to hear me. Even though he didn't look as if he was taking much notice of anything that was going on, I still thought he might be able to hear me. I thought of him lying there unconscious with his mind awash with blackness and scary pictures of tombstones and blood-stained battered lorries. I thought my voice might just come through all that and he might hear it and he'd recognize me talking and I'd be telling him that I wanted him to get better. And that would be reassuring for him and helpful, helping him to feel strong.

I'd even thought of a bit of a joke. We have PE at school on Mondays and it's the football season. Rob hates football. He'll do anything to get out of it. I was going to go up to him in the hospital and sit down next to him and whisper in his ear, "The things some people do to get out of football." If he could hear it, it would make him laugh, make him smile anyway. It would be a nice way to come out of a coma. Smiling.

Anyway, I didn't do that. I sat there for a few minutes feeling uncomfortable. There were some relatives there that his mother obviously hadn't seen for some time and they started talking about things like gardening and how they'd had to leave their dog with their next-door neighbour and they hoped it would be all right. I thought they were just making up excuses for getting straight back home. I think they felt embarrassed. They'd heard that Rob was poorly and they felt as though they ought to come and see him but really they didn't want to know. When they saw how ill he was, they didn't want to talk about it. I was thinking: what if he dies? Where will he be buried? What should we have written on his gravestone? Things like that. If they did think about those things, they never said so. They talked about the patio they were building and I felt really irritated because my father owns this massive DIY shop called *The Joint* and patio doors and double glazing are the main topics of conversation in our house. It drives me mad. My parents make out that they're really benevolent socialists with CND posters and Oxfam pictures on their kitchen walls, but ninety-nine per cent of their conversation is about the price of wallboards and the latest designs in scalloped garden edging.

So I just sat there feeling stupid for five minutes, hoping they might all decide to go home and when they didn't, I just left. I couldn't stand it. Going down in the lift I was nearly starting to cry. I don't think I'd have felt like that if

I'd been able to sit with Rob, just the two of us on our own. I'd have been able to feel that I was doing something. I'd have been able to tell him things, even if he wasn't listening. When you have a friend like Rob who you really appreciate, it never occurs to you to tell him so. You don't keep saying things like, "Rob, I really like you. I'm ever so glad that you're my friend." I suppose I tried to show it by making him tapes and doing things that I thought might please him but when I thought he might be dying, it seemed really important to tell him how much I liked him. How much I'd enjoyed just having him around. I was sorry that I didn't have the chance. In spite of what the nurse had said, I still thought he could be dead next time I saw him and that's why I felt upset. Tears started welling in my eyes while I was in the lift and I felt a bit embarrassed. I was glad to get away.

What happened the next day is difficult to explain. I was really upset at school. I was trying not to worry but I had that scary, nervous feeling in my stomach like you get before you take an exam. I found it hard to concentrate in class. A first year boy bumped into me in the dinner queue. It wasn't his fault but I got really angry. I knew it wasn't him that had upset me – it was Rob, but there was no way I could explain. I suppose that I was feeling upset and worried and I took it out on him. I felt like that all day.

I was still feeling depressed when I got home. Really miserable. I kept thinking about the hospital. It was with me all the time. Lots of people die in hospital. The people who work there know that and they have to keep laughing and making jokes. They have to be bright and breezy like telling me that Rob was getting better and not telling me he was dying. There was nobody there that I could talk to and tell them how I felt.

I had a shower. I stayed in the shower for ages. Normally I just have a wash and get out but that evening I stayed there scrubbing myself and letting the hot water pour over me – as hot as I could stand. I wallowed in it. Somehow I found it comforting – hot water, rinsing over my body, washing away all the smell of hospital and sickness.

After I'd had the shower, suddenly – and this is really difficult to explain – for some reason, I started feeling happy. No, happy's not the right word. I felt elated. I couldn't understand it. I tried to squash it back inside me because it didn't make any sense. It's hard to cope with feelings that don't make sense. I knew I should still have been sad because nothing different at all had happened; but bubbling up inside me was this terrible sense of elation – a sense of elation and joy. It burst out from me and I started singing.

We have these stereo speakers in the bathroom. They play the music from the Dolby downstairs. There was the radio on, playing a record requested by a little girl. It was called "Bright Eyes". It was a record I enjoyed when I was little because it comes from this film called *Watership Down* and it's about a rabbit who dies. It's sort of nice and sentimental. I found myself singing at the top of my voice to the record on the radio.

Bright eyes, burning like fire
Bright eyes, how can you close and fail
How can the light that burned so brightly
suddenly turn so pale
Bright eyes.

I was singing it while I dried myself and while I was getting dressed. Then I put on clean clothes. I put on clean underwear and socks and I got a freshly ironed shirt from my wardrobe and my best new trousers. I felt as if I were going to a party, not visiting my dying friend in hospital. I felt really fresh and good and clean and I put the smell of the hospital into the linen basket with my dirty clothes.

I was still singing when I went downstairs. "You've cheered up," my dad said. I felt guilty because I didn't ought to be cheerful but still I couldn't stop myself.

I went out of the house then to the bus stop. It was a

lovely winter evening – a bit frosty. The sky was beautiful and clear. I ran all the way down the road, springing like a wallaby. I felt wonderful. I kept on singing:

There's a fog along the horizon
a strange glow in the sky –
and nobody seems to know where you go
and what does it mean – oh, oh,
is it a dream?
Bright eyes, burning like fire . . .

I got on the bus and sat looking out of the window at the darkened trees and the stars and I felt as though all of them were on my side – supporting me. Making me feel happy.

I tried to focus my mind back to Rob. I was trying to calm myself down a bit. I didn't want to walk into the hospital singing at the top of my voice. I started wondering – what if Rob did die? What would it feel like? For him, I mean, not me. When I was in the Infants there was a little girl called Carol who sat next to me. One morning we were making Noah's Ark animals out of Playdoh when she suddenly said to me, "My nanna's gone to Heaven."

I'd never heard of Heaven. I thought it must be a seaside resort like La Palma where you go on holiday. "Oh," I said. I couldn't understand why she looked so miserable about it. "Where's that?" I asked her.

"Where's what?"

"Heaven."

"In the sky."

"Oh."

I was making an elephant out of Playdoh. I was more interested in rolypolying its trunk than hearing about Carol's nanna but obviously she must be somebody very special if she had a job as an astronaut, so I asked politely, "How long has she gone for?"

When Carol just sniffed instead of answering, I asked her, "When's she coming back?"

A few minutes later Carol started sobbing. Miss Westlake told me off for upsetting her and I felt very confused.

When I got back home I asked my mum where Heaven was. "It's like a fairy story," she explained. "It's something the church has just made up to try and make people do as they're told. They tell everybody that if they're good they'll go to Heaven when they die and live happily ever after."

I ate my dinner and thought about it. "How does anybody know?" I asked my mum. "People who die don't come back and tell us what it's like, so how do we know if they've gone to Heaven or not?"

She couldn't tell me that.

When I walked inside the ward, the nurse was just taking the black mask away from Rob's face. "Are you staying for a bit?" she asked me.

"Mmm," I nodded. I don't know what she thought I'd come for if I wasn't going to stay.

"His mum's just gone to get a cup of tea," the nurse said. "She'll be back in five minutes."

It was good to be able to sit with Rob but the joke about football didn't seem right any more.

I wasn't sure what to do – now that we were on our own.

His hand was lying on top of the covers – the hand that had a plastic tube leading into it, so I just touched his hand. I felt a bit uneasy because it was something I wouldn't have done if he'd been conscious, but while he was lying there in a coma, it seemed all right.

"Rob," I said. "Rob . . . ?" I sort of patted his fingers a bit. There was no movement in them at all. I really wanted to get close to him. I sat on the side of the bed even though I know you're not supposed to do that in a hospital. I felt like putting my arm around his shoulders but I was scared of touching his head with all the bandages and tubes so I just rested my hand on his shoulder.

"Rob . . . " I whispered. "It's me . . . Julian." When there wasn't any answer, I urged him gently, "Come on, Rob, wake up . . . "

When I think about what happened next I get a lumpy feeling in my throat. What happened was that Rob's eyelids moved just a little tiny bit. They flickered and then they opened. At first his eyes just stared out into space as if Rob didn't know where he was or what was happening. Then I pressed my fingers on his shoulder. "Rob . . . " I said again. I don't think he moved his head but he turned his eyes towards me and I could see that they were focusing. He looked straight at me. He looked at me and tried to smile. It wasn't a great big grin or anything, just a little wrinkling in the corners but I knew that it meant that he'd seen me and that he knew who I was and it was his way of letting me know.

I smiled back at him and then I squeezed his hand. Not too hard because of the tube contraption. I can't really claim that he squeezed my hand but yet he definitely moved. There was certainly some pressure of his fingers on my hand. Rob took a little gasp then; he made a sort of gargle in his throat. His hand began relaxing slowly in my grasp. I couldn't see his face at first because my eyes were misted up. I took a tissue off the locker top and wiped my eyes with it and then, when I looked back at him, I saw that his eyes were clouding over. That's the only way I can describe it. I noticed then that he'd stopped breathing. Perhaps I should have shouted for the nurse; but I didn't. I wanted to see what was going to happen next. Anyway, I don't think she could have done anything and I didn't want anyone else to come because it was so important. Just me and Rob and my holding his hand while his body went limp and the strength went out of his fingers. I didn't want other people to intrude. All I wanted was to sit there. His eyes really faded then – they went glazed and hard and I knew that must be how you can tell when someone's dead – like in the song, his eyes were growing dim.

It was beautiful. I didn't feel sad at all. I felt privileged to be with him, proud to be the person who had sat with him while he died. It was the loveliest thing that had ever happened in my life. I wasn't tearful because I was sad – but because it was moving; that was all.

Then I heard the curtains open and I turned round and there was Rob's mother with the nurse. I didn't know what to say to her. I know you're supposed to say, "I'm sorry," because that's what they say on television and on films. I tried to say it but all that came out was a stifled choke and that's when I found myself crying. I'd have been all right if I hadn't tried to speak.

Rob's mum and the nurse both put their arms round me but that only made things worse. The nurse passed me some more tissues, patted my arm; then Rob's mother cuddled me. She wept then as well.

Then the nurse asked me if I'd like a cup of tea. I thought that was very kind of her. I thought as well that it might have been a tactful way of edging me out so that Rob's mum could sit at his bedside on her own.

The body was starting to look less and less like Rob. It seemed completely lifeless now. Like a waxwork. I decided it was time to drink my tea and go.

I didn't catch the bus back home – I walked. It's only a couple of miles but I needed the time to be on my own and to think. I thought a lot of nice things about Rob – I thought about some of the good times we'd spent together and I didn't worry at all about the selfish things like who I would find to play Monopoly with next week.

The other thing that I gave a lot of thought to was to wonder why I'd suddenly felt so happy in the shower. When Rob was in pain I'd felt him crying out to me – that was when I'd heard him screaming in my head. I felt very strongly and I can't explain this but I felt certain it was true – I felt as if it was still Rob's thoughts that I was picking up. When Rob was dying he wasn't in any pain and he didn't feel worried or frightened. He had a glimpse of something wonderful – something light and joyful. There was some kind of vision in front of him that took away the fear and made him feel happy and hopeful about dying. I'd somehow picked up a small part of that picture in my mind. I'd just got a tiny glimpse of it. That was how I understood it.

I couldn't believe that Rob had simply disappeared. The most important part of Rob – whatever it was that put the sparkle in his eyes couldn't just have gone out like a burned-out candle. I felt certain that whatever it was that was Rob still existed somewhere. And wherever it was it was happy. The only way I can describe it is to go back to the conversation I had with Carol when I was six years old. If anybody wanted to ask me where Rob was, the only thing I could tell them was that he'd gone to Heaven.

I look up from the file in disgust. I feel sickened. I polish off the rest of my lager and stare at the plastic formica-topped table.

They shouldn't keep files on kids. That's the main thought in my mind. There are laws made to protect kids – protect them from child molesters or working too many hours in factories or shops. They ought to be protected from people spying on them: opening their letters, reading through their diaries, listening to their phone calls. They ought to be protected from people like me.

The stuff this kid has written is personal and private. We're not talking about state secrets here – just things that are secret to him. His private life. I've thought all that through before of course. I don't have any private life. I get snooped on; my details are there on file and data disk. Somebody somewhere must know everything there is to know about me. Perhaps nobody has a life of their own. Not any more.

I walk across and look out of the window, down into the park. The park has children playing on the swings; it has a monument to soldiers killed in action; it even has a little library. An English park. Nothing could be more normal.

They have spy satellites now which operate from Menwith Hill. They can see inside your bedroom, the way I'm looking at the children on the swings. Except that they can see much closer. They can tell what book you're reading, even which page of the book. All of us are spied on. None of us know when.

I sit down again at the plastic-topped table and turn over to the next page of the file.

* * *

SUBJECT: CHRISTOPHER

A few days after Rob died, they held a service for him in the church. I took the morning off school and went down on the bus. I didn't know what to expect. I was still feeling stunned.

I knew there would be lots of people there – like those in the hospital who'd sat and stared at Rob with all his bandages and wires as if he were a monkey in a spaceship. Great-aunts and second cousins who hadn't seen Rob for years but felt as if they ought to be there because he was family. I hoped nobody would ask me again if I was family. I thought they might make me sit on my own at the back.

It was the first time I'd been inside a church. It was old with polished wooden seats and stained glass windows. There weren't many people there; only the first few rows were full. I went and sat down near Rob's mum.

In front of the bench was a ledge with hymn books and prayer books and bibles. Hanging in front of me was a sort of cushion with floppy ears; I noticed some people had taken theirs down and were kneeling on them. It seemed a good idea to stop your knees from feeling too cold on the hard stone floor. I took mine down as well but I didn't kneel on it straightaway. I sat and looked round the church and listened to the organ music. I thought it was very nice.

The service was difficult to understand even though it was written down. The vicar kept missing out bits so sometimes I'd lose my place and then find we'd moved on a couple of pages; then the hymns were in a different book and the Bible readings in another. I spent a lot of time just finding where we were up to. In spite of that I thought it was very good. I especially liked the part where the vicar talked about Rob. I didn't think he knew him all that well. I'd never known Rob say that he'd met the vicar, but he seemed to have found out a lot of things about Rob and he said them really well.

The vicar said that there were very few things in life we could be sure about. Most people there, he said, probably weren't too sure about the church and the Bible and about

God. When we did feel sure about things, like our political ideas, we often changed our minds when we got older. One thing we could be sure of though, he said, was that all of us were going to die. We didn't know when it would be, but it would happen to all of us one day. I knew it was obvious, really, but I'd never thought of it like that.

None of us came with any guarantee, the vicar said, that we were going to live a certain length of time. It wasn't God that decided when we were going to die; it was chance. It could be on our way home from church, or the next day, or in another fifty years' time. Nobody knew. But what was important, he explained, was not how long we lived but how good our lives were and what we managed to do with them. All of us could do our bit, he said, to make the world a brighter place and make other people feel happier and richer for having known us.

I started feeling sad then because that's just how I felt about Rob – that my life was richer for having known him. Then the vicar talked about Rob and said how he felt sure he'd brought a lot of joy into the world even though he'd died so young. Rob's mum started crying then; she started sobbing into her hanky. That made me feel weepy. I didn't cry out loud, but I felt as though I might have done if I hadn't been with so many people I didn't know. The vicar said that some people might think Rob's life was wasted because he'd never grown up and got a job or had a wife and children. That didn't matter, he said. It was better that there weren't those people there to grieve for him – just his parents and his relatives and friends. I felt pleased I'd got a mention. It made me feel less of an outsider.

We finished with "Amazing Grace" but hardly anyone could sing it properly because most of them were crying. After that we had to kneel on the stuffed cushions with ears to say some prayers. The vicar said some, then there was a quiet time for us to say our own. I'd never said any prayers before. I didn't really know what a prayer was. They said prayers in assembly at school but I wasn't allowed to go because my mum and dad were atheists. I sat in the library with the Jehovah's Witnesses and Muslims.

I didn't really know who I was supposed to be praying to or what I should be praying for. I started off by saying, *Oh, Heavenly Father*, because that's how the vicar had started off but I couldn't remember what he'd said next. I looked around and everyone else had their heads resting on their hands and Rob's mother had her lips moving as if she were talking quietly to someone, so I thought I ought to try again.

I thought about Rob and wondered if there was anything important I wanted to say about him. Then I realized: yes, there was. I put my head down on my hands and said the thing that was most important in my mind. I didn't say *Heavenly Father* this time. I just said, *Thank you*, and then, *Thank you for Rob. It was really nice having him around.* And then I said *Amen*, because that's how the vicar had finished all his prayers.

Then I looked up at the stained glass window at the side of me. The winter sunlight was filtering through forming dusty golden rays. The picture on the window was of a man with long blond hair and a flowing brown robe and sandals. I thought at first that it was Jesus but then I remembered that he was a Jew so I thought he'd have to be dark, not blond. At the bottom of the window was some writing. The letters were very old-fashioned so it was difficult to make them out, but when I did they read: *Come unto me all ye that travail and are heavy laden and I will give you rest.*

I didn't understand what the words meant. All I knew was that reading them made me feel elated, like the way I'd felt in the shower just before Rob had died. The words made me think of somewhere peaceful and refreshing like a cool lake in the summer. I felt as if the words had given me a vision. A vision of how things could be. I kept reading them over a few times so I could keep them in my mind.

After I came home, I kept thinking about the service. I decided that some of the things I'd learned in church were more important than what they teach us at school. I'd learned, for instance, that I could die at any time. I know that's obvious, but I'd just never thought of it before. When the vicar had said that what was important was not how long our lives were, but what we did with them, it made me think that, if I got knocked down and killed tomorrow, I wouldn't have achieved very much. I didn't even know what it was I wanted to achieve. I hadn't even started thinking yet what life was all about. I thought that perhaps I ought to start getting a move on.

My mum and dad never talk about religion. They have the same attitude towards the church that some people have about sex. They treat it as a dirty word. Whereas I know some parents get worried if their kids don't go to church or read the Bible, my mum and dad are always going on about why I haven't got a girlfriend yet. They make me feel inadequate because I don't have sex. I didn't bother about it much when I was only thirteen or fourteen but now I'm in the fourth year, it sometimes makes me worry in case I finish up being left behind on the shelf.

My dad started talking about it the other week for what must have been about the twenty-third time this year. We were finishing off our vegetable curry and with one breath he said, "Pass the pitta bread across, Julian, will you?" And with the next he said, "I hope you don't think sex is anything to be ashamed of . . . ?"

I tried not to sigh too loudly. "No," I told him. "No, I don't think that."

He wiped the wholemeal pitta bread around the remnants of his curry. "People have too many hang-ups about sex," he went on. "It's a very beautiful experience."

I nodded enthusiastically.

"You know, we've always tried to give you the kind of creative environment where you could develop liberated attitudes."

I tried to wrap my fork around a welter of lentils and brown rice, forcing myself to take a peanut with every mouthful. I don't like peanuts in curry.

"There's nothing you can't talk to me about, Jules, you know . . . contraception, masturbation . . . any problems you might have . . . you know that, don't you?"

"Yes." I knew. I watched my father finish off his curry and wipe his fingers on a napkin, hoping he'd shut up.

"Did you read that book I got you?"

"Yes," I nodded grimly. *All You Need to Know About Sexually Transmitted Diseases*. It had turned my stomach over. It's no use insisting how beautiful sex can be then giving me books filled with pictures of incurable genital sores and oozing pus.

"What did you think?"

I thought that if sex was likely to turn my private parts into the festering abscesses in the illustrations, then beautiful experience or not, I'd prefer to spend the rest of my life in a monastery. "It was very, er . . . very useful."

When I was in the Juniors in Mrs Johnstone's class I used to be in charge of tidying the book corner. I remember a series of books that I liked because they had numbers on the top right-hand side and I liked to line them up in order on the shelf. They were all to do with health care and had titles like *Mark Goes to the Dentist, Fiona Has some new Glasses* and *James Gets a Hearing Aid*. There was even one called *Pauline Has Nits*. I remember that because there was a girl called Pauline in our class and people kept pretending that the book was about her and everyone pulled faces at her whenever they passed her table.

Nowadays they probably have health care books called *Simon Has Syphillis, Harry Contracts Herpes* and *Pauline and John Go to the Special Diseases Clinic*. The kids in Mrs Johnstone's class now are probably reading *Fiona Has an Abortion* or *Mark and James Have Oral Sex*.

My dad poured himself some grapefruit juice. "Well, if you ever have any problems in that direction, Jules, just let me know. I can make you an appointment at the clinic – I've been there myself, you know. I'd be happy to take you along."

Both my parents try really hard to be trendy. I know my dad would really like to be able to mention to his friends that he'd been to the Special Clinic with his young teenage son, but I can't help it if I never need to go there.

It isn't because I'm not normal that I don't have sex. I don't think so, anyway. I feel randy sometimes just like anyone else but I find the whole situation with girls and going out with people really awkward. I don't feel ready for it yet.

I did try and have sex once and it was awful – really embarrassing. I decided to wait until I was a bit older before I had another go.

What happened was that I got invited to a party by this girl called Clare who's in our class at school. I'd never been very keen on Clare but she'd told several of my friends that she wanted to go out with me and had been writing my name on the inside of her folders – that sort of thing. I think all that's a bit immature myself, but anyway, I'd never done anything to give her any encouragement so I was a bit surprised when she came and invited me to this party. I asked her what date it was and said it was very nice of her to ask me but I thought I might be busy. I was a member of the Young Communist League and they were having a public meeting which I was hoping would turn out to be on the same night as the party. I told Clare I'd let her know.

Afterwards I started feeling guilty. I thought how hard it must have been for Clare to just come up and ask me to go out with her – for all I knew she could have been hyping herself up for it for weeks and be really disappointed if I turned her down. It wouldn't do any harm, I thought, just to go with her to a party – it didn't mean I had to go out with her again or anything. The Communist Party meeting turned out to be the week afterwards so when Clare asked me again I said OK. I thought I'd done the right thing because she looked so very pleased.

When I got to the party I changed my mind. I don't know

what I was expecting – not jelly and cakes and Hide and Seek; I'm not so stupid – but I thought there would be things to do. I'm happy just to have a dance and chat to people but it wasn't that sort of a party. Everybody was in couples and they were lying on the settee and on the floor and under the table in various stages of intimacy and undress. There was no way to engage them in conversation. I just had to sit down with Clare in an easy chair in a darkened corner of the room, put my arm round her neck and start kissing her.

At first, I didn't find it sexy. Just very uncomfortable because the chair was cramped and we didn't have too much room. I'd never kissed a girl before and I was hoping it didn't show. I tried to remember how I'd seen people kissing on television and in films. They usually did it standing up and it seemed more difficult sitting squashed in an armchair because I didn't know where to put my hands. I tried to stroke her hair and things like that but my arm kept getting stuck. I felt embarrassed when somebody put the lights on because I thought I must have looked really stupid and clumsy. Clare seemed more experienced. She kept putting her tongue inside my mouth and stroking her hands along the insides of my thighs and I found myself feeling sexy. It came as a surprise because I thought you only felt like that with girls you found attractive. I never thought I could get turned on with a girl like Clare.

Then I started to feel uncomfortable. There seemed to be this pressure building up inside me; I wanted to press myself against her and move my hips around and, of course, there wasn't room for doing that squashed up on the armchair. I didn't know where to put myself. Part of me wanted to just freak out and go home but a part of me that seemed a lot more powerful was saying: Yes, I'm kissing a girl and it feels OK and I want to carry on and have sex and enjoy it. The trouble was that I didn't know how to progress; I didn't know what the next stage was.

Clare knew all the different stages. When I was getting

really passionate, she started licking the inside of my ear and then she reached forward and whispered, "Shall we go to bed?"

It didn't seem right to me in somebody else's house but Clare apparently was a very close friend of the girl whose party it was and she said it would be all right. She led me into the hall and upstairs into this girl's bedroom.

Inside she closed the door. Then she took her jumper off and lay down on the bed. She was wearing nothing at all underneath her jumper. I lay on the bed beside her. I'd neither seen nor felt a girl's naked breasts before. I'd seen hundreds of pictures of them and I'd always thought they looked attractive but feeling them was nicer. They felt firm but soft and cuddly. I got really excited. I liked the way her breasts just fitted inside my hands and I started stroking them and squeezing them.

The next thing was that Clare started making little moaning sounds. That's what really got me. She started making these lovely little purring sounds like a kitten stretched out by the fire. Then she started making little tiny groans of pleasure. It was really nice. It made me feel so excited to think that I was turning somebody on and making them feel as though they wanted me. I got really worked up then. I lay on top of her and started grinding my pelvis against the tightness of her jeans. It was all too much. What happened next is something I feel really embarrassed about. I curl up when I think about it. I just felt myself coming. There was no way I could stop myself. There I was, lying on top of her, fully dressed and I didn't know what to do. I thought about standing up and taking my trousers off and getting inside her before it was all too late but I knew it would have taken much too long. There was no way I could hold back.

I rolled off Clare and cuddled her while I throbbed away inside my pants. Then I started kissing her and all the time I was wondering what to say. I couldn't think how to explain. When I'd calmed down and subsided I told her I needed to go to the toilet. "I'll be back in a minute," I told her. "Don't go away." That was a really stupid thing to say because I'd have given anything to come back and find she'd disappeared.

There was a queue outside the bathroom. There always is at parties. I felt really self-conscious, holding myself and wondering whether anyone could see the dampness spreading round my crotch.

Inside the bathroom I wiped myself down and thought about what to do next. I wondered how long it would take me to get aroused again but I'd no idea; it could be hours. The big temptation was just to split the scene and go home but I thought about Clare lying in bed panting for me and it seemed too awful just to go home and leave her.

In the end I went back inside the bedroom and told her I had to leave. "I'm sorry, Clare," I told her. "It's all been really nice but I'll have to get off home. I've to be up early in the morning."

It's a good job it was dark so I couldn't see the expression on her face. "My mum's coming round to fetch me later on," she said. "She'll give you a lift back home if you want her to."

"That's very kind," I said, "but I don't want to put anybody out."

I felt as though the least I could do was to kiss her goodnight. I regretted it straightaway because she locked her arms around my neck and started dragging me back towards the bed. I had to work really hard to get disentangled. "It's been really great, Clare," I told her. "Thanks for inviting me. I'm sorry I've got to go."

I ran out of the door and down the stairs like a spring-loaded Matchbox car.

I place the first part of my report on his desk. Everything is written up neatly and efficiently. I pride myself on working well.

"If I could offer an opinion, Sir . . . ?"

He looks up at me and raises an eyebrow.

"I'm inclined to disagree with whoever's been working on this before."

He says nothing.

"The subject seems to be OK. It seems to me we're wasting our time with him."

The Boss just nods. I was expecting him at least to glance at my report. He doesn't even bother to open the smart imitation-leather-backed executive display folder. He never even sees my subject dividers, each with its rectangular white sticker labelled neatly in Letraset. He could at least look at it and grunt, *Yes, that looks fine. Thank you. Well done.*

He frowns. "Well, we've got the rest of the family under observation. The mother's been to Greenham Common; the father has sent timber and equipment there. The whole family has visited the Soviet Union on more than one occasion . . . "

There must be thousands of people every year who go to the Soviet Union but that doesn't make them Russian spies. I nod politely.

"Anyway, let's see . . . you're only investigating two other people, aren't you? Can't you cope with this as well?"

I'm not suggesting I can't cope. Just telling him it's unnecessary. "Yes, Sir, I can cope."

"If he does seem 'clean' as you say, then we'll just keep him on file until someone more important turns up." He gazes absently at the potted dock leaves in the corner.

What he seems to be saying is that, because we have people who play at spies, then there have to be people to spy on. We have to find people that are suspect. And the number of suspects varies according to how many people we have who want to play at spies or how many we can afford to pay. I think it's absolutely ridiculous.

"I suppose . . . that sounds logical, Sir."

He nods. "We'll reassess the situation when I come back from leave. Give it another three or four months."

He passes me a torn brown envelope that has been used half a dozen times already. "Here's the rest of the first part of the file."

* * *

I finished up telling my dad that I'd got a girlfriend. I regretted it straightaway but it seemed harmless at the time. It happened because after Clare had invited me to the party she told everyone else in the world apparently that she was going out with me. I think I was the only person alive who hadn't been informed that the two of us were supposed to be going steady. Clare's not what you'd call one of the most attractive girls in the school and, to tell the truth, she does have a reputation for being something of an easy make, but there was no need for Simon Wincklass and Mark Lancaster to warn me quite so often about the dangers of catching AIDS, leprosy, herpes of the throat and gonorrhoea. I've found out from experience that if you just ignore people when they're trying to rile you, then pretty soon they just give up. But before Simon and Mark gave up, they took my Tipp-Ex out of my bag and drew a huge white heart with an arrow through it on the back of my Social Studies folder and wrote *Julian loves Clare* inside it. I brought my folder home that afternoon and threw it into the waste bin in my bedroom.

My dad noticed it straightaway when he came in my room to borrow back his new Bruce Springsteen album. "So, you've fallen in love, Jules . . . " he said.

I tried to repress the groan that had fast-forwarded from nowhere into my throat. It came out like a strangled belch. "Oh, I wouldn't say that," I told him.

There was a pause for a couple of seconds but obviously my dad was just dying to find out. "Is it somebody at school?" he asked me.

"Mmmmmm."

It was the next question that caused all the problems. I should have seen it coming over the horizon by the casual way he started playing with my new Atari joystick. "Have you been to bed with her then?" he asked.

If I'd had any sense I'd have told him to mind his own business; it had nothing to do with him. But of course I didn't. I suppose there was a part of me that wanted to please him or impress him and I knew that given the situation – because I'd been to the party by then – I could say that technically I had been to bed with Clare without telling an actual lie.

I nodded.

My father's face lit up. He had the same look of pride as when I assembled my first DIY bedroom storage unit. He positively glowed. "Great!" he said and patted me on the back. I felt a bit guilty then because I knew I hadn't done it properly and I could see all kinds of problems arising like my mother phoning up Clare's mum and suggesting that she make her an appointment at the Family Planning Clinic, but it was too late then. I'd said it.

A few days later my mum was driving me into town and she mentioned about how my dad had told her that I'd got a girlfriend and if I'd like to invite her back for the night sometime that would be quite all right by her. She said it casually as if the thought had only just occurred to her, but it was obvious from the tone of her voice that it was really well rehearsed.

I just nodded. "Thanks," I said. I tried to think of ways of explaining the situation but it seemed easiest not to bother. To me that part of my life ought really to be private. Even if I did have a proper girlfriend and was sleeping with her all the time so I didn't have anything to be ashamed of, I still don't think I'd want to tell my mum and dad about it. I think I'd rather keep it to myself.

After Rob had died, I tried a couple of times to go back inside the church where they'd held the funeral. Both times it was locked. I felt disappointed. When I was there for the funeral I'd wanted to look around at all the statues and the stained glass windows and things but it didn't seem right to be too inquisitive. It seemed as though that was something I'd have to do on my own. When I went back I looked around for a noticeboard saying what time the church was open but they didn't seem to have one.

Anyway, there was a little graveyard by the side of the church and the second time that I was there, I decided to look at the graves. It was quiet, like a sanctuary. There were squirrels chasing across the grass and a pair of chaffinches hopping by the hedge. You could only just make out the shape of some of the headstones because they were covered in ivy. From a distance it looked as though someone had thrown a rough green blanket across them. There were gnarled and knotted tree roots pushing through pieces of stone edging. Even though a lot of the graves were so old they were breaking apart, I didn't feel frightened. It was much too nice and peaceful to feel scared.

I walked along reading the headstones. Whole families were buried there with parents and grandparents and their grandchildren. There were marble urns and carefully-carved scrolls and little statues. One grave had an angel reading a book carved out of stone and inside the book was written *Blessed are the pure in heart; for they shall see God.* Another grave had a figure carrying a curly-haired child on its back. Below it read:

In precious remembrance of our darling Sophie
Dearly loved and only child of
William A. and Nellie Roberts
Aged 4 years
Fell asleep at St Annes-on-the-Sea, October 17, 1918
"God was one day gathering flowers
And on his way He gathered ours."

There was a little plot near the bottom hedge which had a tiny wrought iron fence around it. It was covered in grass and weeds but there were crocuses just peering through. It made me realize then that it must be the start of spring.

I went over to look at the crocuses and then I noticed an urn buried in weeds at the back. I could just make out the inscription: *Come unto me all ye that travail and are heavy laden and I will give you rest.*

I stopped and stared. I felt a bit shaky as if something important was starting to happen, but I didn't know what it was. It was like hearing a tune that brings you out in goose-pimples and you don't know why. You start to wonder if you might have heard it before somewhere. Of course I did know where I'd heard the words before because they were written on the stained glass window in the church. I thought at first that they disturbed me because they reminded me about Rob, but it wasn't just that. I remembered the vision I'd had. Something like a cool lake in the desert. That was the picture that I had. I also had a feeling of taking the oasis with me. It sounds stupid to say it like that but that's the only way I can describe it. I looked down at the crocuses just showing streaks of colour through the shoots. The words and the vision were just giving me a glimpse of how things could be, like seeing the first hint of colour on a crocus. One day, I thought, when the season started to unfold, it would spread the colours out.

When I got home I decided to look for a bible. We have thousands of books at home. My father's built storage units up to the ceiling in three of the downstairs rooms and there are shelves of lovely books, most of them bound in leather in matching sets. My parents get them from book clubs. None of us ever read them but they do look smart. "They'll be really useful for your education, Jules," my father said. "You never know when you'll need to look something up."

I waited until my dad was cleaning the car because I didn't want him to ask what I was looking for. I felt sure we ought to have a bible somewhere. Unfortunately his Radiophone started paging him and he came scurrying back to the house.

"What are you after, Jules?" he asked, sprinting towards the study.

If I'd wanted the kiss of life I don't honestly think he'd have given me enough of his time to risk missing out on a new contract or an order. I started muttering something but by the time the words came out he was in his study taking the call.

He passed through again five minutes later. "What are you looking for?" he asked me.

"I wanted something on religion."

"Well, let's see, we've got the Qur'ān, *Zen and the Art of Motor Cycle Maintenance, Jonathan Livingstone Seagull*; we've got some books on yoga . . . "

"Have we got anything on . . . " I hardly liked to say the word, "on Christianity?"

There was an awkward silence. My father looked confused. "Mmmmm . . . we've got *Religion and the Rise of Capitalism*. I've not read it myself but it's supposed to be good. It's a bit heavy going." He took down the leather-bound volume. "Is this a school project or something?"

I nodded slightly. I didn't want to lie to him but I didn't know how to explain. "Have we got a bible?"

He shook his head and pulled a face. "No."

"It doesn't matter, then," I told him. "It's not important."

"Are you sure?"

"Yeah, it's OK."

He went back to polishing the chromework on his Lotus.

In the school library I looked up Bible under subjects but there was nothing there. Then I went to the author index. I'd no idea who'd written the Bible so, of course, I didn't know who to look up. I looked up Jesus first and he wasn't in and then I looked up Christ but he wasn't in either. I didn't think God had written the Bible but I couldn't think of anyone else who might have; so then I looked up God in the Dewey system and of course they didn't have any books by him at all. I realized then that was stupid. The Bible was supposed to be all about Jesus and God – not written by them, but in that case, who did write it?

I asked the librarian but she didn't seem to know. "Why don't you ask Mr Finningly?" she said. "He's head of RE.

He should have lots of bibles."

I expected to find the head of Religious Education in a kind of monk's cell leading from a cloister. I found his office by the home economics suite, warm and cosy with the smell of home-made cakes and coffee. Mr Finningly sat behind his neat and highly polished desk. He wore a natty little suit and a tie which had a crown on. I always thought that meant "By appointment to the Queen". He motioned me to an undersized chair near the door.

"I wondered if you could help me," I started.

He looked up briefly. "Mmm?"

I had intended explaining to him all about Rob and the funeral, what I thought about the service and about the inscription in the graveyard. I'd been through it in my mind and decided I really wanted to discuss it all with someone else.

Mr Finningly had opened one of his files and was skimming through a list of names. It's not easy to explain things that are important to somebody who's reading something else. "I've been wanting to sort of... educate myself," I went on clumsily.

"Mmmmm..."

"I wanted to find out about the Bible and about Jesus and everthing."

Mr Finningly looked at me and frowned. "It's not an easy subject," he said. He glanced back at his file again. "Are you in my group?" he asked.

"No."

"Oh." He looked a bit cross about that. "Well, that's why I can't find you on my list. Well," he closed up the folder and looked at me properly for the first time, "Religious Education is a difficult subject. It's not an easy option as some people seem to imagine."

"I didn't think..." I started, but he wouldn't let me carry on.

"Some people choose Computer Studies because they

think that will be an easy option. Then when they find that computers mean hard work, they ask to change over to RE. We want people in RE lessons who are there because they mean to work."

"I'm sorry," I told him, "I don't want to do RE in school; I just want to read the Bible and find out about God and everything."

Mr Finningly gave me the look of someone who'd just found out that I'd been wasting his time.

"I tried to find a bible in the library. The librarian said you might have one."

He did look cross then. "We have twenty-eight bibles here." He indicated a pile of them on his shelf. "One for every member of the class. If I just gave out bibles to anybody who asked me for one, then those people who *really* want to study the subject would be flummoxed. Wouldn't they?"

I nodded. What offended me was the way he'd said *really*. What he meant was that if you weren't taking an examination then there wasn't any point in finding out about something. I resented that.

"Well, I'm sorry to have taken up your time," I said as I stood up.

"You wouldn't ask the Geography teacher if you could borrow an atlas for a few weeks whilst you went on holiday . . . "

"No."

"Or ask to take a school computer home to play with . . . "

"No."

"Our budget's been cut by thirty-three per cent this year. We haven't bought any new text books for the last eight months. I have to stay behind in the evenings repairing them with Sellotape."

I nodded sympathetically.

"Trying to erase some of the obscenities that you lot choose to scribble on them."

That made me feel quite angry because I'd never scribbled obscenities on a school text book in my life. I thought about explaining to him but it didn't seem to be worthwhile.

I think I'm getting somewhere. It might be too early to say that, but that's the way I feel. Things are starting to unravel.

Last week it would have been Rob's birthday. I tried not to think about it but the date, May 7th, had a circle round it on my calendar and I kept seeing it coming up. The more you try not to think about something, the more it seems to haunt you.

May 7th was a lovely spring day full of sunshine and the shopping precinct was filled with people out in their summer clothes. There were flower stalls at the side of the road; there were flowers blooming in the tubs outside the Wimpey and McDonald's and there were flowers in the shops. I felt like buying some flowers first and then I thought afterwards about who I could buy them for. You can't just buy them for yourself. It was then that I thought about Rob's mum. She must be more upset than I was that it was Rob's birthday and he wasn't around to enjoy it, so suddenly I thought that I would buy some flowers and take them round for her.

I'd been meaning to go and see Rob's mum. I'd told myself that I'd call in on a Saturday and see if she wanted any jobs doing or just make sure she was all right. I never had. Then, because it had been such a long time, I'd felt too embarrassed to go round. Anyway, I bought three bunches of different coloured tulips and persuaded myself that she'd still be pleased to see me even though I'd left it so long that she might have forgotten who I was.

Rob's house (I can still only call it Rob's house even though he doesn't live there any more) is completely different from ours. It's very small and all the furnishings are worn and comfy. The chairs are sort of bent into people's shapes and you can tell where the carpet has been walked on because there are patches where the pile has worn away. My mum and dad would hate that. If any of our furnishings show the slightest sign that anyone has used them, they replace them straightaway.

Rob's mum looks worn and comfy as well. I know that

sounds rude but I don't mean it in an offensive way. I think it's nice. She has greying hair and wrinkles and wears clothes that make her look cuddly. My mum would hate to look cuddly. My mum has her hair streaked once a month at Antonioni's and gets upset if the roots show even half a centimetre. You hardly ever see what her face is really like because she hides it with foundation and blusher and things called camouflage sticks. Her clothes are always chic and expensive. She does have casual clothes – for jogging in and cutting the roses but even those are trendy – like flying suits with lots of zips and stretch towelling track suits. That sort of thing. I'm very fond of my mother but it was nice that Rob had a mother who was completely different and I could like her a lot as well.

I walked down Rob's path with the bunches of flowers. Part of me was hoping that his mum would not be in because I suddenly felt shy and awkward and guilty that I'd not been back. Everything was familiar but it was familiar because of Rob. If you have a cupboard that your favourite toys were in and then they're not there any more then you don't want to open the cupboard door. You don't want to have to come face to face with them not being there. That was how I felt about the house where Rob used to live. I knocked on the door and waited.

It was a long time before anyone answered. Rob's mum didn't recognize me straightaway. "Hello," I said. Then, when she hesitated, I added, "It's me, Julian."

She seemed really pleased to see me. "Julian," she said. She pronounced my name as though it were Prince Charles. "Haven't you grown? Come in."

I never know what to say to people when they tell me that I've grown; I suppose I must do it all the time but I never notice it myself. "I've brought you some flowers," I told her and offered her the tulips. I was glad to get rid of them actually. I'd been carrying them for half an hour and the stalks were sweating in my hand.

She took them from me and smelled them and started

saying things like, "Oh, you shouldn't have," and, "They must have cost a fortune." I wished she wouldn't. I have my own charge card and bank account and I think it's awful that people who are so much older than me don't have a fraction of the money that I do.

Anyway, Rob's mum steered me into the front room. That's the room she always keeps nice and tidy for visitors. It smelled musty as if it hadn't been used for a while. When Rob was around we used to chat with his mum in the kitchen while we drank big mugs of coffee. It seemed funny to go back there as a visitor who sat in the best room.

Rob's mum went to make some tea and brought it to me in a china cup with little biscuits on the saucer. We chatted a bit but at first it seemed really awkward. She asked me how I was getting on at school and how my mum and dad were and how the business was going. It seemed as though neither of us wanted to mention the one thing that was really on our minds which was the fact that it would have been Rob's birthday. To make it worse, there, on the sideboard, was a birthday card. Just one. I tried not to look at it but the more I tried to veer my eyes away, the more they kept coming back. It had a footballer on the front and that was really strange because Rob always hated football. I couldn't believe that anyone would have sent him a card with a footballer on but I couldn't understand who else it could be for. It certainly wasn't for his mum.

There were quite a few pauses in the conversation. Not long ones because whenever there was a silence one of us would fill in quickly with some trivial comment or a question. It seemed as though both of us were avoiding any mention of Rob and that seemed really sad.

In the end I gave up trying to be polite and just stared at the birthday card. Rob's mum turned round to see where I was looking and then she went to pick it up. She held it out to show me. "I don't know if you know anything about this boy . . . " she hesitated. "It's somebody he used to write to in France. A penfriend. I thought they'd stopped writing to one another, until this came . . . out of the blue . . . "

I knew Rob had had a penfriend ages ago. We all had them in the second year after the French teacher gave them out but most of us had stopped writing after the first few months. The only ones who'd kept it up were those who were hoping to get a free holiday abroad and that's what I suppose had happened. This French boy was thinking he might be able to come over on an exchange if he got in touch with his correspondent again. I reached out for the card. "I'll take it to school if you like," I told her. "I'll ask the French teacher if he knows who Rob was writing to. I could send him a note in French and let him know what's happened."

I wasn't sure if my French vocab was really up to explaining how his pen pal had been knocked down by a lorry but I thought the French teacher might help me out.

Rob's mum looked relieved. "Well, I don't want to put you to any trouble," she said, "but it would be a load off my mind."

Now that the birthday card had cropped up it seemed safe to talk about Rob. I turned the card over in my hand. "He always hated football," I said and both of us smiled.

It seemed to have opened something up because Rob's mum started talking then about Rob, a long, long stream about him. She said that there were things in his room that she'd just left, but there were things other people might like to have, like his tapes and his records. I offered to help her sort them out sometime. "Whenever you feel like going through them," I told her, "just let me know and I'll come round."

I didn't say much but I enjoyed just sitting and listening to Rob's mum. She said that although people had been kind and considerate, most of them just never mentioned Rob. "It's almost as if he never existed," she explained. "I don't want to think that people have forgotten him already."

"I'll always remember him," I told her. I thought then about what the vicar had said in the church. "It's made my life better for having known him," I said.

She seemed quite moved by that. She talked away for another twenty minutes or so and then looked at the clock and started to apologize for having kept me. "You must have lots of things to do," she said. "I didn't mean to go rabbiting on."

"That's all right," I told her. "It's been good to have a chat. It feels nice to come back here."

Rob's mum sighed. "Well, that's very kind of you," she said as she stared down at her empty cup. "It's not been such an easy day for me."

"No."

"This morning, when the card came, I looked at it and at first . . . at first it seemed like a joke . . . a sick joke someone was playing. Sending a birthday card. I realized it was ignorance – it wasn't his fault. He didn't know that Rob was . . . I sat down and had a little weep and I couldn't pull myself together. I thought I'd finished with all that."

I nodded. I could see why she felt upset. "Haven't you had anything from the doctor?" I asked her. "My mum always goes on Valium when she gets upset."

Rob's mum shook her head. "I wouldn't take things like that," she told me. "When things seem to be getting too much . . . I just say a little prayer."

It seemed an odd, touching sort of thing to say. I imagined how my mum would react if I suggested she say a little prayer instead of reaching for the tranquillisers next time life got her down.

"And something always happens to cheer me up," she explained. She glanced towards the flowers on the sideboard. "Like those tulips. I can keep looking at those this afternoon."

I found it hard to believe that anyone could be cheered up by something as simple as a bunch of flowers. Maybe there was something for me to learn from that. I thanked her again for the cup of tea and the biscuits. I decided not to leave it quite as long before I came round to see her again.

FILE JC110
SUBJECT: CHRISTOPHER

Yesterday my father gave me four packets of condoms. I nearly choked on my muesli. He'd just handed me the form to take back to school.

Please send me the following number of tickets for the Parent-Teacher Association German Sausage Evening.
Herren und Frau at £6.50..............0....................
Jungen at £4.50..................................0....................

That's hardly surprising because all of us are vegetarian. But then he said, "Here's something else for you, Jules," and gave me a little wink. Then he presented me with four packets of condoms. I didn't know where to put myself. I mean, at least he could have left them in the chemist's bag. I put them on the table next to the marmalade. *Sensuola*, it said on the packets. *Ribbed for heightened sensitivity*. I cringed. I felt the eight pairs of eyes from the ecstatic couples on the packets stare at me as I munched my way through my croissants.

At school I gave them to Simon Wincklass. He's the Simon who wrote *Julian loves Clare* on my folder that started all the fuss in the first place. He's always going on about how many girls he's screwed so I thought he might find them useful.

Halfway through the afternoon, I was called into the deputy headteacher's office. I walked in feeling really cheerful because I'd just come out of Computers and the program I'd been working on for the last five lessons had turned out really well. I'd constructed it for my dad to use at work. It was for the customers when they first came into *The Joint* to key in the size of their rooms and the kind of materials they wanted – paint, wallboarding, floortiles, wallpaper, etc. – and it would work out how much they needed to buy. I'd had to put a lot of work in beforehand, finding out how many tiles you'd need to cover a bathroom wall and things like that; but my dad said that would be really useful for me for when I joined him in the shop. When I'm old enough he wants me to be a director.

As I walked along the corridor, I started singing a few bars of the advertisement I'd already made up to go along with the new Customer-Assistance computer. There's a song called "Big Spender" that has a line *Whenever you walk in the joint* – that was the beginning of it. My advert started off with Madonna looking absolutely fantastic standing outside the store's automatic doors singing, *Whenever you walk in The Joint* and then beckoning people inside to show them me, personally demonstrating the new computerized Customer-Assistance Program.

I was still singing to myself as I strolled into Mr Burfield's office. I stopped dead in my tracks as I saw him glowering at me. By his side was Miss Mallinder, the new art teacher and . . . horror of horrors . . . I could hardly believe my eyes . . . hanging over the edge of his desk, like bedraggled socks on a washing line, was this row of soggy condoms. They just sat there, dripping on to the floor. I didn't know where to look. It was so shocking I wanted to laugh but when I looked up at Mr Burfield's purple face glaring across at me I sensed that I was going to be in trouble.

I stood meekly in front of Mr Burfield's desk. I know you're not supposed to sit down when you're being told off but standing up was really difficult because I didn't know where to look. I couldn't look at the new art teacher because she seemed more embarrassed than I was; I couldn't look at Mr Burfield's irate face with steam flowing out of his nostrils because if I did I would have cracked out laughing and I couldn't look down at the row of soggy contraceptives because then I'd have folded up in hysterics.

I remember once in Drama a teacher told us that if you looked just over somebody's head, they would think you were staring them straight in the face. Just above Mr Burfield was a poster of a pig with a notice saying, To Know Me Is to Love Me. I decided to concentrate on that.

Mr Burfield used to be an officer in the army. He often tells us about it in Maths. Instead of talking, he either grunts like a walrus or bellows like a sergeant major.

"Well . . . ?" he bellowed at me.

I couldn't think what to say.

"You have some explaining to do . . . *Christopher!*" He snarled my name as if it were something he'd found hanging on the end of one of the condoms.

I did tell him once before that Christopher is my surname – not my Christian name, but he nearly went berserk. "You have two names, boy!" he roared at me. "I shall call you by whichever I find the least objectionable."

There was an unpleasant silence.

"Certain second year boys," explained Mr Burfield in careful measured tones, "saw fit to fill these disgusting objects with water and squirt them at female members of their class in this afternoon's art lesson."

I could see then how they'd got so wet.

"I have been told that you are the lout responsible for bringing these filthy items into school."

I didn't want to say yes to that. Firstly, because I don't consider myself a lout and secondly because although I find condoms a bit embarrassing, I don't see any way in which they can be described as filthy.

"Well?!"

"My father buys me contraceptives," I explained as sensibly as I could whilst gazing at the massive pig's snout on the wall. "He seems to think I enjoy a more active sex life than I do and I happened to have a few spare. After that useful talk on contraception last week in Social Studies I thought it would be sensible to share them out. It seemed wasteful to throw them away."

Mr Burfield glared at me incredulously. "If your father thinks it right to give his children contraceptives," he snarled derisively, "then that's a family matter, but that doesn't mean we have to put up with that filthy corruption spreading to innocent children in the school!" He paused. "If children are allowed to smoke at home then that doesn't give them the right to bring cigarettes to school and dole them out to all the first and second years."

I felt tempted to explain to him that cigarettes are harmful to children whereas contraceptives aren't.

"Does it?"

Of course he didn't want to know what I thought about it. This wasn't a conversation; it was just a play we were in. The script was written a long time before I walked in through the door.

"No, Sir."

"Nor is it any reason to cause so much offence to one of our lady teachers."

My mother tells me off for saying lady. She says that all women should be called women, or womin as she spells it. For all I know, Miss Mallinder might be more offended by being called a lady than by finding condoms in the art room.

"No, Sir."

"Well I hope you're going to apologize."

"I'm sorry, Miss."

She nodded her head at me, the first thing she'd done to acknowledge the fact that I'd walked inside the room.

"Well . . . " said Mr Burfield, "what are you going to do about it . . . ?"

The only thing I could think of doing was to find Simon Wincklass and tell him what I thought of him. "I don't know, Sir."

"What you want to do is grow up."

The other week in Maths Mr Burfield sent out Darren Simpkins for flying a paper aeroplane. "Go and stand out in the corridor!" he roared. "Until you grow up!"

Darren's still not old enough to start shaving so I assume that he's still standing there.

"Stop playing childish pranks. You're in the upper school now, boy."

(If ever I'm late for school, my dad brings me in his Lotus. The other week, as we were coming down the drive, Mr Burfield marched in front of us slowly and deliberately so my father had to almost stop. When my father tried to pass him, he walked in the middle of the drive, making it impossible to overtake. I thought that was very childish. My father was furious.)

"Well, you can take this lot with you."

He pointed to the row of condoms. I didn't have my bag with me and they were too wet to go in my pocket so I just had to hold them in my hand. I didn't screw them up. I just dangled them between my finger and thumb as I strolled out into the reception area. Unfortunately I walked straight into a row of prospective pupils and their parents waiting to see the headmaster. I tried humming the tune to "Big Spender" to help me look cool and relaxed but it came out as a muffled squeak. I couldn't even recapture the picture of Madonna standing by the doors.

My father kept on buying me contraceptives. I started to feel a bit upset about it because I didn't know what to do with them. I daren't give out any more at school but also, I didn't want my mum or dad to come across the dozens of unopened packets I'd secreted all over my bedroom. I wasn't too keen on Janet, the cleaning woman, coming across them either. I put some down the waste disposal unit but I regretted that straightaway because I realized that they could have clogged it up. You're not supposed to put anything down that's made of plastic or rubber.

I did sneak some in the dustbin, wrapped in several layers of brown paper and scrunched inside an empty tin of curried chick-peas with the lid squeezed down; even then, I was worried on the day when the bins were emptied; there's always at least one tin that falls out of the lorry and gets pounced upon by next door's cat. I dreaded coming home and finding the empty curried chick-pea tin rolling down to meet me with its contents spewed all over the drive.

The other thing I considered was to use them. After my dreadful disaster with Clare had faded into the realms of distant memory, I decided that I really ought to be more adventurous; I shouldn't let one fiasco put me off women for ever.

There was a girl in my class at school called Kerry Ann. I realized that I was becoming quite attached to Kerry. She'd helped me with my computer program for *The Joint*, pointing out a few mistakes that I wouldn't have noticed on my own. We'd spent a lot of time chatting over lunch and we'd been to play badminton together; usually we'd made up a group of mixed doubles so I hadn't spent all that much time with Kerry on her own; but I felt I was becoming fond of her. I found her very attractive – she had a pretty face and a lovely body and the sight of her long, slim legs in her tiny badminton skirt had quite aroused my desire to get to know her better. I decided to take the plunge and try to develop the relationship.

I decided to invite Kerry back home for a meal. That was

fairly stupid because, what I really would have liked would be to spend some time on my own with Kerry, away from the computers and the badminton court to give us a chance to get to know each other. Instead the need to convince my parents that I did have an attractive girlfriend just took over, so instead of inviting her out, I asked her round for dinner one Friday evening.

I didn't regret anything at first because my parents were so very kind and helpful. My father spent ages making us a meal; he brought out some of his best wine from the cellar and both he and my mother really went out of their way to make Kerry feel at home. I was pleased about that; it was one of the few times when I found myself feeling proud of my mother and my father.

After the meal had been cleared away and we'd stacked everything into the dishwasher, my mum and dad decided to go for a walk. I knew they must have planned that in advance. They never go for walks. Especially in the dark. My dad said how he'd just been out with the garbage and noticed what a lovely starlit evening it was and asked my mother if she fancied a stroll to the clubhouse. I know they did mean well, but I wish sometimes they could be a little less dishonest.

"Perhaps Kerry Ann might like to see your new videos," my father hinted as he ushered my mother out through the front door.

Kerry Ann didn't particularly want to see my videos but we went upstairs and played some tapes and a couple of computer games. After we'd finished that she asked me how often the buses ran and what time the last one was. Her mother had driven her round to our house but Kerry had told her that she'd make her own way back. I hadn't expected her to be going home on the bus. I'd expected either that she would stay the night or that my father would drive her home; but my parents hadn't come back yet. I didn't know what time they'd be home.

It was then that I made my second big mistake. I think I was a bit charged up with the wine. It was my father's best wine and I wasn't used to drinking quite so much. I was feeling full of myself and buoyant. I decided to ask Kerry Ann if she'd like to stay the night. When I say decided, that's probably not the right word. If I'd thought about it, I would have seen the dangers looming up, but I didn't think about it; I just said it. I asked her nicely; I thought I did anyway. I rested my hand gently on her shoulder and gave her a little peck around the ear.

Kerry Ann hesitated for a moment. She held my hand and looked at me. "Is that what you want?" she said.

That's when I made my next mistake. I felt as though Kerry was looking right into my head; I felt as though she could tell what I was thinking. I was thinking that I wanted more time to get to know her better; I was thinking that I'd like to feel able to talk to her more frankly; I was thinking that I was scared.

I felt ashamed. I was a bloke after all. Blokes were supposed to want to screw women, not sit round talking to them. I put my arms round Kerry's neck and kissed her. "Of course that's what I want," I said.

From then on there seemed to be no turning back. Kerry Ann went to phone her mother, to tell her not to wait up and that she'd be home sometime in the morning. While I listened to Kerry talking on the phone, my buoyancy and elation dropped to nil. I felt sure I'd let myself in for something more than I could handle. I went downstairs to fetch the rest of the wine for us to drink. When I came back with the bottle and some glasses and saw Kerry waiting for me on the edge of the bed, I felt a momentary panic. "Would you like a cup of cocoa as well?" I asked her.

"I'm not bothered," she said. "The wine'll be OK, thank you."

"I think I'll make myself some," I said. "If you don't mind."

Kerry Ann just smiled at me. "That's fine," she said.

I sped down to the kitchen, mixed myself a mug of cocoa and stood it in the microwave. I wanted to keep calm and relaxed. I normally made myself a cup of cocoa every night before I want to bed. It was a sort of routine I had. At one time I used to warm up the milk first and then pour it on the cocoa but my mother complained about the dishwater never cleaning the milk pan properly so I started mixing it first and then letting it heat up. I watched the seconds count down on the microwave: *Five*... I had a feeling of dread in my stomach. It was turned over and wrapped around like an apple strudel. *Four*... I wished I felt more in control; I felt as though the situation was in charge; not me. *Three*... If I'd taken Kerry out to the cinema, I wouldn't be in this mess. *Two*... But there was nothing I could do about it now. *One*... This was it then. Blast Off!

I took out my mug of cocoa and carried it upstairs. It was like a comfort blanket – a little patch of security in a world where nobody could tell me what might happen next.

We sat together on the side of my bed and I struggled to gather my thoughts together and see whether there was any way in which I could talk to Kerry Ann about what was on my mind.

I felt as though what I wanted with Kerry was what people would call a relationship. I wanted us to go out together and get to know one another. I didn't have many really close friends and that sort of companionship was something that I felt I lacked. If I failed completely in bed with her, then I knew that I'd be placing that in jeopardy.

I couldn't think what to say. I poured myself a drink of wine and I refilled Kerry's glass. "Will your mum and dad mind me staying here?" she asked.

"No," I said. "They're very good like that."

I suppose that made it sound as though I was always bringing girls back home to stay the night but I didn't bother to correct myself.

I kissed Kerry Ann again and she put her arms around my neck and cuddled me and I started feeling warm and sexy. It seems to turn me on to know that somebody really fancies me. I thought the most sensible thing to do was just to snuggle down under the duvet together. I smiled at Kerry. "Come on," I said, "let's get into bed."

We took our clothes off at opposite sides of the bed facing away from each other. Perhaps both of us were a little bit shy. Actually, I would have very much liked to watch Kerry getting undressed but, as that would have meant turning round myself, I decided to give it a miss.

The next thing I decided was by far the most fatal mistake of the evening. My main concern was that I'd repeat the same mistake that I'd made with Clare, that I'd find myself getting too charged up, feeling too sexy and coming too soon. What I decided to do to try and stop that happening, was not to think about sex for a while; in fact to concentrate my attention completely on something else. As I took off the rest of my clothes and climbed into bed with Kerry Ann I decided that, instead of letting myself get carried away with the anticipation of making love, I'd focus my thoughts on one of the other current problems in my life.

I put my arms around Kerry and I stroked her hair and kissed her ears. As I did that, I started thinking about the likelihood of the waste disposal unit gunging up. I'd noticed tonight that already it seemed to be malfunctioning. The probability was that my father would have to send for somebody to fix it and he'd find out what had caused the problem and I'd be left with a lot of explaining to do.

Kerry kissed me passionately on the mouth. I ran my hands up and down her body and thought about how I could explain to my father that my contraceptives had finished up down the sink. I thought I could tell him that I'd wrapped them in a plain brown paper bag and then, when I was throwing away my empty Kit-Kat wrappers and so forth – turning out my pockets – they must have just got scrunched up with the rubbish that I was throwing down the sink. I never did like telling lies but it was the best way I could think of to avoid hurting my father's feelings.

Kerry Ann seemed to be feeling passionate. She was working her tongue around inside my mouth and stroking her fingers round the bottom of my spine. It seemed about time to get my mind switched back to making love. Suddenly, I had a horrifying thought; in spite of all the dozens of packets of condoms that were hidden about my room, none of them were within an arm's reach of my bed.

I tried to remember where they were. There were six packets on top of the pelmet; there were some more filed inside my stamp album, under Guatemala; there were two or three inside the cover of an old Gary Glitter LP that I'd bought from a Socialist Workers' Party jumble sale for my mother and then discovered it was Gary Numan she liked, not Glitter and there were one or two others in my bicycle saddle bag, outside in the garage.

There were none within easy reach. I'd no idea what Kerry Ann would think if I suddenly leapt out of bed, stark naked, and started clambering up the curtains, leafing through my stamp collection or searching out my Gary Glitter LP. I didn't know what to do. It was just at that moment of panic that Kerry breathed out, "Mmmmmmmmmmmm," in a huge long sigh, flopped back on the mattress, stretched her legs open wide and muttered, "Oh, Julian. I really want you . . . " and dragged me over on top of her.

I nearly collapsed with shock. Here I was doing everything I could to stop myself feeling turned on and, when it came to the time when I should have been ready, I was as lukewarm as a lettuce. I suppose my body must have suddenly gone completely rigid – most of my body, anyway – all the bits that didn't count. Whatever it was, Kerry Ann realized straightaway that there must be something wrong. Somehow, I think my absolute lack of enthusiasm must have communicated itself to her. "Is there anything the matter?" she asked me.

The next thing she did I don't think I can ever forgive her for. She reached her hand down to my prick – she had a difficult job in finding it actually – and of course, when she did find it, it was as droopy as the skin on my cocoa. And then she sat up and glared at me and said, "Well, if that's how you feel . . . " Then she turned her back on me and shifted right over to the other side of the bed, taking my half of the duvet with her.

I felt mortified. I just didn't know where to put myself. I couldn't think of anything to do and I couldn't think what to say. It all seemed to have happened so quickly. It only felt like two minutes before that we were climbing into bed together. And now I'd spoiled everything. I could hardly believe it had happened.

I sat up in bed and reached out for my cocoa. I needed the comfort and reassurance of a warm drink in my throat. But everything had taken longer than I thought. The cocoa was completely cold and left bits of skin clinging round my mouth. I wiped them away with a tissue from the box I'd left beside my bed in case we might need them later on.

I felt that perhaps I ought to apologize to Kerry Ann; I thought that maybe I'd hurt her feelings and she might be a bit upset. I reached over and touched her gently on her arm.

"Kerry . . . ?" I started gently.

She pushed my hand away angrily. "Leave me alone," she said.

There was something unusual about the way she said it. Her voice was almost normal, but it had a strange note that sounded almost like a squeak.

I felt sad about that. I think the problem was that Kerry Ann was crying.

When I woke the next morning, Kerry Ann was gone.

At first I just assumed that she was in the bathroom, or that she'd gone downstairs to make herself a cup of tea. It was very sad because, when I woke up I was feeling randy. I'd just had this really sexy dream and I lay in bed aching with lust and imagining how I'd make love to Kerry as soon as she came back. Gradually it dawned on me that Kerry

Ann wasn't coming back just then and, the chances were, that she would never come back at all. When I buried my head in the pillow and wept, my tears were a mixture of frustration and self-pity.

I forced myself to get up early. I'd like to have stayed in bed, just feeling sorry for myself but I wanted to get out of the way before my parents came downstairs and started asking me where Kerry was and when I was seeing her again.

I made myself a cup of tea and a slice of toast. I didn't eat the toast. I nibbled at it for a while then shoved it down the waste disposal unit, which still wasn't working too well, and then I put my coat on and went out for a walk.

It was a warm clear sunny day; I needn't have taken my coat. I'd hardly noticed the summer coming on because I'd been busy revising for my A levels and I'd hardly been out at all. I felt angry with the weather. When I was feeling miserable and sorry for myself, it didn't seem right that the day should be bright and sunny, with families setting off in their cars for picnics and little children riding on their bikes wearing nothing but T-shirts and shorts. I'd have felt happier if it were raining.

One of the good things about where we live is that nobody walks about. The houses are large, detached and spaced out and everyone travels by car; I knew there was no chance of meeting anyone I knew.

I wanted to be on my own. Once I started walking, I thought of all the things that I wanted to say to Kerry Ann, and I explained everything to her as if she were walking along beside me. I told her about my parents and how they made me feel guilty about sex; I told her about Clare and how I'd felt such a failure with her; I told Kerry how attractive I thought she was and explained that, even though I hadn't been able to make love to her, that was no reflection of the way I felt about her. Finally, in a scene so poignant that I almost had tears rolling down my cheeks as I walked silently down the street, I eventually confessed to

Kerry Ann how much I loved her and, with all the intensity my imagination could bring to bear, I heard her say how much she loved me and how she wanted to carry on and really try to make a go of the relationship in spite of all the problems that we'd been through at the start.

I started feeling better then. I felt more hopeful. Having told Kerry Ann all that had been going through my mind, it was as if the words had actually been spoken and I started planning then about how we'd make things up and what we'd do together in the future. I imagined us going out for walks together; I saw us arriving at the Christmas disco with Kerry looking absolutely radiant and all the boys in my class at school drooling over her with envy. Once I'd started making them up, scenes like that just went on and on.

Afterwards I wished I hadn't felt like that. I wished I'd just been sad.

When I went to school the following Monday, Kerry just ignored me. Well, that isn't strictly true. When I said hello to her in Computer Studies, she smiled and nodded at me, but then whizzed over to her Commodore in the corner and switched on her new Hangman program for teaching remedial kids to read. I'd helped her draw the hangman with the graphics a couple of weeks before.

Even though Kerry's desk was in the corner, so she wasn't *en route* to anywhere else in the room, I managed to make a detour and pass behind her whenever I went to open a window (twice), whenever I went to the toilet (four times), whenever I went to sharpen my pencil (five times) and whenever I went to throw my screwed-up, wasted work into the waste-paper basket (about twenty-seven times). Each time, I glanced at her monitor and hesitated, wondering if there might be anything I could offer to help her with. To my intense annoyance, she seemed to be getting on all right.

Kerry was making the Hangman program a great deal more elaborate. Whenever the kids came across words they couldn't spell, she wrote GO TO lines which said things like:

Look out! You've had it now! And, Prepare to meet thy Doom!!! And, Death Awaits You!!! Then, instead of just drawing the hangman, she made the program so the noose actually went up and down with a tiny figure inside it. I thought it seemed a bit morbid for little kids; I thought they might get so frightened it could put them off reading for life. I also couldn't understand what it was that had made Kerry Ann suddenly start feeling so sadistic.

"We need the next diary."

I thought that was coming, somehow.

I stare across at the potted dock leaves.

"I'll leave that up to you."

My heart sinks. I ought to be hyped up with the prospect of adventure but I'm not. I find it all totally sordid.

I look across the desk top at my old Boss, the one I've worked for several times before. I don't even know his name. Nobody tells you their name.

"I've been looking at the case," he goes on. "The subject has recently been spending far less time at home. Conventional methods of surveillance are less useful. We have . . . " he pats the file in front of him, "several gaps to fill in since this was written."

I nod.

"I think you're the man to fill them."

I nod again, grudgingly. When I first came out of the army, I thought about setting up in business. I thought I'd like to own a record shop. I like sorting things out and filing them. I could see the records all set out in rows, all of them catalogued. I'd have sold posters and tapes as well. I'd have felt relaxed and easy. I'd have been friendly and chatty with the customers. Nobody would have had cause to hate me.

The Boss is watching me like a hawk. I shift a little in my seat.

"What I think we need . . . " He's choosing his words very carefully, staring me straight in the eye, testing the time to tell me something. I begin to feel uncomfortable.

He lowers his voice and leans across towards me. "What we could do with is a more . . . a more personal . . . " He gives a tiny flicker of a knowing smile. "Someone who could come up with a more . . . *intimate* relationship."

I'm not sure what he's referring to at first. I'm about to nod politely and then I hesitate. He doesn't mean . . .

The knife twists in my guts. I glance up at him, not believing that we're on the same wavelength. The superior knowing smile is frozen on his face. This is just not bloody fair. What right has he got to . . .

"You do know what I mean?"

The bastard. My life. My private life. My private sodding life that has nothing at all to do with this stinking shit of a job. My private life is me – myself – my world which he has no right at all to investigate, to infiltrate, to legislate or even, *I hate him* . . ., to contemplate. Who the hell does he think he is sitting here telling me that I can't have any private life because they know everything about me as if they own me? The bastards.

I feel my fingers tugging at my earlobe. I don't let the expression on my face change one iota but inside my guts are turning over.

I don't know what to tell him. I think back to what he's asked me: *You do know what I mean?* I have to try my best to stay cool. I nod my head in resignation. "Yes, Sir," I tell him, "I know what you mean."

He smiles. That's the answer he wanted. The pervert. "Good. So long as we understand each other."

I want to get out of here. The office is stuffy and claustrophobic. I start to rise.

The Boss glares at me and I sit back down. We have to finish the conversation.

* * *

Ministry of Defence
Main Building
Whitehall
LONDON SW1A 2H8

"D" Notices on British Intelligence Services
and Ciphers and Communications

PRIVATE AND CONFIDENTIAL

File JC 110
Part II

RIVELIN VALLEY CRIMINAL RECORDS

INPUT DATE:	10/05/85	**SEX:**	Male
SURNAME:	Christopher	**FORENAME(S):**	Julian
NICKNAME(S):	none known	**ALIAS(ES):**	none known
P.O.B:	Maidstone	**D.O.B:**	25/12/66

ADDRESS: 7 ("Highgrass"), Windermere Road, Bishopston

STREET TYPE: Upper class suburbia

ABOVE ADDRESS VERIFIED: 01/05/85

VEHICLE(S): none

HEIGHT:	5ft 5ins	**PHOTO NO:**	SB/110/3/27/84
EYE COLOUR:	blue	**BUILD:**	slim
RACE:	white	**HAIR:**	brown
FACIAL HAIR:	none	**ABNORMALITIES:**	none

RIVELIN VALLEY CRO NO: 347/84/110

SECURITY LEVEL: Special Branch

REASON(S) FOR INTEREST: Membership of subversive organizations, parents under surveillance

LAST CONVICTION DATE: no convictions

REMARKS: Membership of Young Communist League from 08/11/80
Membership of Campaign for Nuclear Disarmament (Rivelin Valley Youth Bránch) from 28/01/81
Friends of the Earth membership from 18/03/70 (Family membership)
Greenpeace supporter (Family subscription) 01/09/84)
Sighted: Youth CND stall, Bishopston precinct, 16/03/85 and 07/04/85

Electrofix
Electrical Domestic Appliance Repairs Limited
17 High Street, Bishopston

Mr. J. Christopher
"Highgrass"
7 Windermere Road
Bishopston

3rd April, 1984

Dear Mr. Christopher,

We enclose our account for the servicing of your waste disposal unit.

As your unit is no longer under guarantee and our engineer has been called out twice during the last month, we would like to remind you of the instructions in your manual regarding the proper use of the machine, specifically relating to the disposal of plastic material. It seems that someone has been attempting to unclog the unit apparently wearing plastic disposable gloves which have then become dislodged and caused the resulting damage.

We would advise you to ensure that such articles are kept well away from the unit in the future.

Yours sincerely,

B. Stokes

Mr. B. Stokes
Service Engineer

For the next few days I kept thinking about Kerry Ann. I kept wanting to speak to her and explain things to her and I kept telling myself that if only I could take Kerry Ann on one side and just talk about the way I felt, everything would be all right.

After a few days it seemed obvious that Kerry was just avoiding me. It wasn't that she was rude to me; when we were supposed to be playing badminton, for instance, she told a friend of hers called Marie that she wouldn't be able to play and asked her to come along instead. In the dining-room, where we used to sit and chat, she'd walk past me with her tray and say hello but then she'd go across and sit at a table with someone she hardly knew. I felt most upset one day when she said hello to me and then went and sat at a table on her own. After a while I started feeling more and more rejected. Then it seemed much harder to ask Kerry to go out with me again and, after a couple of weeks had gone by, I suppose I just gave up.

It did occur to me to talk to my mum about it. She'd always said to me that if I had any problems then I should discuss them with her. On some occasions she'd been very helpful – like, for instance, when I was in the first year: some older kids at school were sniffing glue and they kept threatening to beat me up if I didn't bring them tubes of Evostick from the shop. I hated violence – I still do, actually – and I started to get really scared of going to school. I kept saying I felt sick or that I had a headache. My mum sat me down and had a chat about it and then both my parents came up to school with me. I felt terrified. These boys had threatened to do such terrible things to me if I didn't bring them the glue; I couldn't imagine what they'd do when they found out I'd told my parents and the headmistress. But then the head said how sensible and brave I was for saving the lives of people who might otherwise have died with their heads inside plastic bags and their lungs all clogged up. The kids had to apologize to me then go and be counselled at a special centre. Within two or three hours the problem was solved and everything was all right again.

I knew it couldn't be like that with Kerry. It was no use staying off school, pretending I'd got tummy ache; it was no use asking my mum and dad to come up and tell the headmistress about her. It was no use making Kerry Ann apologize and there was no point in sending her off to be counselled. Kerry didn't like me; that was that. If she'd been really fond of me then she'd have wanted things to work out; she wouldn't have just let one little problem put her off.

Anyway my mum had her own life to cope with. She kept visiting the women's peace camp at Greenham Common and taking them firewood and stuff to make their benders – like little wooden tents they lived in. When she came home, she went to meetings, raising money for the peace camp and persuading other women to go down and help them out. The peace camp was important; it was about saving the world from nuclear annihilation and I didn't want to have to take her time up with trivial problems about my state of mind.

Another thing that happened about that time was that we had a burglary. There was nothing stolen because my father heard a noise and came downstairs and whoever it was ran off. Even though nothing was missing, my parents were very upset. My mother found it hard to sleep at night because she kept imagining that there was someone creeping round the house. Sometimes it was just the wind and once it was a cat that had got locked inside the garage. The doctor gave her tranquillisers to take before she went to bed but in the mornings she looked drawn and tired. I didn't want to bother her with problems of mine as well.

One thing that was strange about the burglary was that I lost my diary afterwards. I didn't tell anyone about it because I knew that a burglar wouldn't steal a diary but I couldn't think where it had gone. Anyway, I didn't mention it. I didn't want anyone to know I kept a diary. I wanted to keep it private. That's why I decided to buy this new lock-up diary with a key.

Anyway I just tried to accept the fact that, at that moment, I felt deeply hurt and rejected and there was nothing I could do. But, for some time, I just felt really low and depressed. The situation with Kerry was the main reason but there were other things as well. It had reached the stage where we only went into school when we had exams. It was drawing near the time for me to leave.

I'd actually been looking forward to leaving school since the day I first started at four and a half. Most of the others in our class were worried about finding jobs, or they were worried about whether their qualifications would be good enough to get them into college or university. I didn't have anything like that to concern myself about. My job had been lined up for me since well before I was born.

When my dad first started training me in the business, we owned a fairly small DIY shop. When I was little, he taught me to sort out the nails, cut little bits of wood or fill up the empty shelves. I loved the smell and feel of the timber when it had just been cut and planed. I liked to meet the customers as well. Because it was a local shop, you got the same people coming in. They used to bring me sweets and biscuits and make little jokes with me while they waited to be served.

All this time, my dad was looking out for what he called a big investment. Finding *The Joint* came as a fantastic breakthrough for him. It was a disused factory in an area where the new Windermere housing concept was starting to be developed. My dad had a friend on the local council who helped him get planning permission to turn the decrepit old factory into what they described as "an exciting new concept in home refurbishing". He mortgaged everything we owned, he persuaded the bank and several of his friends to lend him as much as they could afford; it was a fantastic gamble but it worked.

Basically it was just a massive DIY shop, but it was architect designed with an open-plan staircase and a gallery.

It had a pine-clad coffee bar with its own pump-operated waterfall; it had slides and climbing frames to keep the kiddies occupied and had potted plants and designer wall-paper everywhere you looked. It even had its own 1960s juke box. We had sales staff trained in interior design who offered people on the new housing estate a complete service, redesigning their homes with everything from our shop. We started to make a packet. Before too long we bought one of the poshest houses on the new development; we swapped our old transit van for a Range Rover and a silver Lotus sports car, we employed over forty staff and had all the cash we needed.

By the time I was ready for leaving school my future was all mapped out. I was learning to drive, I understood the computerized stock system, I was on friendly terms with all the staff and I'd already made my special new computer program for the shop. In some ways, everything was wonderful. What had started getting to me was that I had never actually sat down and thought about what I wanted to be when I grew up. What if I found out when it was too late that I didn't want to be a director of *The Joint*?

I woke up one morning and felt a need to get away. I didn't know why I was going but I went out into the country.

I have a bike, a racer that I hardly ever use. My dad bought it for me one Christmas along with all my other presents. It had got to the stage where they'd bought me just about everything that parents buy for their teenage sons and the only thing that I didn't have was a bike. There was quite a good reason for that: I'd never wanted one. My dad thought that because Rob had a bike, I'd probably like to have one as well. What my dad didn't realize, because he'd hardly ever spoken to Rob, was that Rob's bike was a BMX and the one he bought me was a racer so we could never really go out on them together. I used the bike at first to go to the shops or to go to school on when I'd missed the bus but, after a couple of months, it just stayed in the garage.

So I suddenly had this urge one summer morning to set out into the country on my bike. I felt quite excited. I'd spent so much time lately at home, or helping my dad in the shop, that I'd almost forgotten how nice it was just to get away. I put a can of fruit juice in one pocket and an apple in the other; I wheeled my bike out of the garage, checked its tyres, gave it a bit of oil, then I was off.

I couldn't understand why I'd never been to the country on my own before. It was great. It was a sunny day but not too hot and there was a slight little breeze. Just to stop me sweating too much. It's fairly flat near where we live, just occasional hills, nothing very steep, so I was able to cover fifteen or twenty miles without any hassle at all. I didn't know where I was going. I set off and rode through some villages, past cute thatched cottages and a church or two and then I stopped at a village post office and bought myself some cans and a couple of packets of crisps; I'd got through my apple and fruit juice within the first ten minutes.

After that, I came to this heathland with gorse and heather and little streams. It was beautiful. I sat by the side of the stream where I could see right to the hills in the distance and then I ate my picnic. I'd never been anywhere so quiet. I could hear the stream gurgling below me; there was a bird hovering and singing like a black dot high up in the sky – I think it was a skylark – there were a couple of shaggy sheep munching their way past, but apart from that, I was completely on my own.

The countryside was something that I'd hardly known about before. I'd known that it was there. We'd had lessons at school about wheat production and how tadpoles turn into frogs; but I'd never realized before that things in the country were so much to do with life. Nearly everything at home was to do with making money and keeping the house looking nice. Everything was artificial. Maybe that's why my mum and dad were so keen on eating natural food and drinking fruit juice. They had so few things in life that were absolutely real.

I started thinking then about the other things that had been on my mind. I still had strong misgivings about starting work at *The Joint*. I knew I ought to be grateful. I knew I was lucky to have a job and a family business to move into. I just wasn't sure whether that was what I wanted to do with my life. The thought of it was oppressive. It was like a mould that I was being poured into. I'd started to see a picture of myself a long time in the future, with my own architect-designed house, just like my mum and dad's, with a dishwasher and a flashy car. And later on, my own son, constructing DIY units in his bedroom, preparing himself for the mould that would make him a director of *The Joint*.

I finished my crisps and shoved the screwed-up packets into my pocket and then I climbed a little way to the top of an outcrop of rock that was higher up the stream. I looked across to the hills where they blurred together in a hazy mist on the horizon and I wished there was someone I could talk to, someone who could help me.

I had been trying really hard to find something positive in life. When I was in my early teens I'd joined the Young Communist League. A bit later on I'd left that and joined the Socialist Workers' Party. Neither of them had been right for me.

Since Rob died I'd made an attempt to understand religion; I hadn't done much about it recently because I'd been working so hard for my exams. I felt as though there was something there for me but I didn't know how to approach it. Religion wasn't as straightforward as the Young Communist League had been. You didn't just pay your subs and fill in a card and join.

I wanted to pray. I didn't know how to do it because I wasn't sure whether I believed in God or not. I didn't see how I could pray to someone if I didn't know who he was or whether he was really there.

Then I remembered what Rob's mum had said. She had told me how she prayed whenever life was getting her down. Life was getting me down at the moment. I thought I might give it a try.

I looked across to the hills. I hesitated. I didn't know what to say. As I paused, I had a feeling of . . . a feeling that what I was doing was important. I felt a bit shaky, almost as if I was going to cry. I didn't cry. Instead, I said quietly, "Whoever you are, please help me." And then, "Tell me what to do." I waited and thought for a moment. "Please show me," I went on. "Please tell me what to do."

Then I closed my eyes. I don't know what I expected. Maybe I was waiting to hear the voice of God booming out of the hillside like an underground loudspeaker. Or see a vision of glittering angels, parading across the heavens like a Hollywood chorus line. What happened was better than that. I felt flooded with love. That's the only way I can describe it.

I sat still with my eyes closed. I didn't do anything. I just felt the love sweep over me. It was as if my body was bathed in love. For the first time in my life I experienced absolute peace and joy.

After a while I got to my feet and walked further up the hill. The feeling of love was still with me; I thought that after a few seconds it would go; but it didn't. It stayed with me. I walked up beyond the gorse and heather to a larger outcrop of rock. I scrambled up it, the last part on my hands and knees. I was out of breath when I reached the top. There was a long, long drop below me but I walked to the edge and looked over; I could see for miles. I could pick out the little villages that I'd ridden through on my bike; I could see the winding pathway and the rocks where I'd stopped to have my picnic. I had a wonderful sense of freedom.

And that's when the awareness came, as clear as the open view. All my life I'd been hiding inside a cage. I'd accepted barriers round me that dictated who I was, what I should do and what I should believe in. What I'd done was start to let the barriers fall down. For the first time in my life I was saying: Maybe. Maybe the impossible is the possible; maybe the unlikeliest things are probable. Maybe I can start my life again. I can break down all the parts and I can build them up again. I don't have to be the way I am if I don't want to. I can change. And the capacity for change is endless. All I have to do is to let down the walls, break up the barriers and expose myself to whatever lies ahead.

The feeling I had was similar to the night Rob died – when I was singing in the shower. I felt elated. When I'd tried to understand the happiness that I'd felt for Rob, all I'd been able to say was that it seemed like what people meant when they talked about Heaven. It was heavenly. What I felt now was that breaking down the walls that had enclosed my thinking – that would be heavenly as well.

I ran down the hill in the sunshine with the wind blowing gently on my face. I hadn't sorted anything out and I hadn't made any plans. I didn't know what lay in front of me but, whatever it was, I knew that now I would find the strength just to rise up and meet it. The Julian Christopher that lived before had almost disappeared and in his place was someone powerful with love. For the first time in my life I felt completely free.

A few weeks later I joined the Radical Christian Fellowship. The reason I first went was because of an article in the *Weekly Gazette*. It was underneath a picture of someone that I'd worked with on a CND stall in the precinct a couple of months before. He was easily recognizable because he had a shaved head and wore gold ear-rings which is quite unusual for a vicar.

By the side of the photograph it read:

PACIFIST PARSON AT PEACE CAMP

Rivelin's radical reverend, Roger Brooks, was charged today with committing criminal damage at Astonbury US base in Oxfordshire. Together with three other members of the Radical Christian Fellowship Roger was accused of cutting a hole in the wire of the perimeter fence, entering the base and spray-painting "LOVE THINE ENEMY" on the runway.

All four members of the group have been released on bail. Back at his post today as chaplain at Rivelin Polytechnic, the radical reverend told us: "I'm prepared to go to prison over this. I understand the law about criminal damage but Christians have to acknowledge an even higher law – the law of Jesus Christ which tells us not to kill and to seek to love those who persecute us."

After I'd read the article, I thought I'd really like to try out this Christian Fellowship. I wasn't sure where they met, so I phoned up the Polytechnic and asked to speak to Roger. He remembered me from the stall in the precinct and he was really helpful. He told me all about the group and where they held their meetings. He didn't seem to mind my interrupting him at work.

I went to my first meeting two weeks later. It was held in one of the rooms at Roger's house. I say *one* of the rooms because it was such a rambling ramshackle house.

We started off by sharing a meal together. I didn't know I was supposed to bring food, but everybody else pressed on me more bread and cheese, slices of quiche, date squares and fruit than I could possibly eat.

When we'd finished, we had to introduce ourselves. There were about fifteen of us; I can't remember everyone's name but there was another vicar called Mark who was plump and jolly; there was a girl called Cathy who looked about my age; there was a Quaker couple called Adam and Meg, and Andy who had vegan-style hair – short at the top and the sides and with a long strand at the back. There was another girl I'd met before called Debra who used to come to Youth CND.

Then we had a time of worship. People said prayers or read out from the Bible. Cathy started singing and everyone joined in. We sang, *Make me a channel of your peace, Where there is hatred let me sow love.* I liked that one. Then, *You can't kill the Spirit, she is like a mountain.* After that we stood up and joined hands and said together the blessing that the vicar had said at the end of the service in church.

It felt cosy and . . . I was going to say friendly but I think the word is *intimate*. It gave me a close warm feeling to share something so important with people that I really liked.

Afterwards Roger and Andy talked about what happened when they'd been arrested at the base and the group made plans for a vigil outside the courthouse when the case came up again. They were going to print some posters saying Love Thine Enemy and one problem was that they wanted wood and hardboard to make placards to stick the posters on.

The obvious thing was for me to ask one of my father's van drivers to deliver them some off-cuts from *The Joint*. We have lots of spare stuff like that and my dad would have been only too pleased to send it. He used to send pieces of wood to Greenham for them to use for firewood. I opened my mouth to offer, but then stopped. I sat and kept quiet instead.

While they discussed the vigil, I gazed about the room. Roger's furniture looked like the sort they leave outside junk shops overnight in the hope somebody will have nicked off with it by the morning. The wallpaper was muddy fawn with faint pink splodges which could have been roses, vomit or the residue of someone violently shaking the tomato ketchup. The only decent items of furniture were the bookshelves which overflowed with tattered magazines and paperbacks on religion, politics and peace. Each one looked as if it had been read by about twenty different people.

The carpet looked smoother than the oil-stained mats my father put down on the garage floor, the only sign it had of a pile being a centimetre layer of dog hair. The dog lay asleep in front of the gas fire, curled into a shaggy snoozing comma of matted fur.

At first I felt sorry for Roger. I thought they must pay him hardly any money as a vicar and it must be a real shame that he couldn't afford to buy any proper furniture at all. Then I looked at all the books and realized that they must have cost him quite a lot and it made me think again. I thought that maybe Roger had different ideas from most of the families on Windermere Road about what things he thought were important. Maybe the problem wasn't that he couldn't afford an Artex ceiling, concealed lights and double glazing. Maybe he just didn't want them.

After the meeting a few of us went to the pub. I talked to Rog and Andy about the action at the US base and the rest of the time I spent with Cathy. She'd come from Leeds to study Art at the Poly where Roger worked. I felt as though I got on well with her. She wasn't what you think of as conventionally attractive; she was a bit plump and I thought she really wore a bit too much make-up and jewellery. She had six rings, about twelve wire bracelets and two chains round her neck. She had a red stud through her nose, a row of little hearts in the top of her right ear and then long feathers threaded through her earlobes which looked like the remains of a long-dead parrot. I tried not to keep staring at them. What I liked about Cathy was that she was so bright and bubbly; her eyes sparkled when she laughed. You felt happy and cheerful just because you sat next to her.

I bought the first round of drinks but no one would let me buy another one after that. I wanted to tell them I could easily afford it but again, I found myself keeping quiet.

I thought about it when I went home on the bus. Normally, I'd take a taxi because the buses only run every fifty minutes. A taxi drove past as we came out of the pub, but I let it go and walked down to the bus station with the others.

It wasn't that I was ashamed of my home and family but somehow I wanted to disown them. I didn't want to ask one of my father's van drivers to deliver off-cuts of wood for the Christian Fellowship because that would mean telling them that my family owned *The Joint*; I didn't want any of them to see me driving home in a taxi; I didn't want anyone to ask me where I came from because the Windermere development is the most expensive part of town. The strange thing was just how much all these things mattered.

The little service had meant a lot to me; it felt really good to meet other Christians who shared the same ideas as me. I didn't want them to think that I was different. For the first time in my life I wanted to be accepted by a complete group of other people. No, I didn't just want them to accept me; I wanted to be like them. I wanted to join in with them, share in the things they were doing and feel at one with the group.

I think that's what made me decide that, before I was very much older, I would probably have to leave home.

In the end I did tell the people in the Radical Christian Fellowship about my parents, where I lived and all about *The Joint.* I knew that even if I did leave home, people would still ask about my parents and whereabouts I was from. I'd either got to talk about it straightaway or tell lies about it for ever.

At the next Fellowship meeting, Roger talked about an idea he'd had for a project. This was just after a report had been published by the churches about poverty in the inner cities and it was something that the group really wanted to do something about. He knew of an unused building owned by the church in Rothwell, a deprived area in the inner city. He asked the church authorities if they would let us use it for projects that would help the local community. They seemed only too glad to get it off their hands.

At the planning meetings Rog was full of ideas: he wanted to turn the building into a refuge for battered women, a drug rehabilitation centre, a citizens advice bureau, a crèche and a peace centre. We managed to persuade him that it couldn't be all those things at once. In the end, we decided just to have some offices for the Radical Christian Fellowship and an advice centre.

We thought that would be enough to start off with: somewhere to keep a filing cabinet, desk, typewriter and duplicator. We thought that once we'd got established, we might start screen printing and have a badge-making machine and perhaps publish our own newspaper. We'd also run an advice centre where we'd help people with basic skills like filling in their application forms for social security and we intended asking congregations in the more well-to-do parts of town to give furniture and old clothes that we'd pass on to people in need.

So on Saturday morning I gathered together a zinc bucket, a couple of mops, scrubbing brushes, a packet of disposable dusters, a litre of white gloss paint and a bottle of disinfectant. I put on my oldest painting overalls, picked up my gear and strolled out to the bus stop singing, *Make me a channel of your peace; Where there is hatred let me sow love...* maybe a bit too loudly for Windermere Road but feeling proud of myself for starting to make a contribution to the spreading of happiness in the world. That was until my dad passed by me in the car. The silver Lotus screeched to a halt. I noticed the horror on my father's face at seeing his son trudging round the streets like an itinerant cloak-room attendant. "Where are you going with that lot?" he asked me as he whirred down the electric windows.

It was a windy day and my nose was running. As I put my mop in the other hand to get my hanky out, I dropped the bucket. It clattered noisily as it started to roll down Windermere Road. My father winced.

"To the bus stop," I explained as I raced down the street after the bucket.

"You can't get on the bus looking like that," he grumbled when I came back. "Get in the car."

He took out his copy of the *Financial Times* and spread it on the seat.

I put my stuff in the boot but there were a dozen reasons why I didn't want my father to take me. I wanted to go on my own. I hesitated.

"Where are you off to?" he asked.

I told him the name of the church but he didn't know where it was. It wasn't the part of town where anyone ordered their kitchen and bathroom units from *The Joint*.

"You can show me the way," he said. "Get in!"

We drove along in silence. From the corner of my eye, I could see my father's moustache quivering frantically the way it does when he's angry. I thought he would switch on the radio or stereo – the silence seemed so heavy and oppressive; but he didn't.

Part of the trouble was that I'd been helping him in *The Joint* on Saturdays. He'd come to rely on that because the shop had been under pressure recently, with lots of staff on holiday. The night before, I'd left him a note saying that I was busy this Saturday. The fact that I was obviously doing some work for someone else was what seemed to have made him mad.

I asked him to drop me round the corner from the centre, but he insisted on driving me right to the door. Fortunately, there was no one around. I thanked him and got out. He said nothing. He just slammed the door and drove off.

I set to work feeling worried and upset, but my mood changed straightaway when Cathy breezed in. She was dressed in an artist's smock, an ethnic multicoloured headscarf, gypsy ear-rings, scarlet tights and a pair of Doc Marten boots. She climbed up a rickety ladder and started emulsioning the ceiling singing, *You can't kill the spirit; she is like a mountain; she goes on and on.* She was an inspiration to us all.

Just before lunchtime Andy turned up. He knew nothing at all about painting. He made such a mess of the walls that Cathy told him to go and paint the toilet out the back instead. Half an hour later he made us all a cup of tea and we decided to take a break. They sent me to the Chinese chip shop across the road with an order for four bags of chips, two pancake rolls, mushy peas and a carton of curry sauce. I'd never realized before that it was possible to buy a meal for four people for less than £3.80.

We sat on old newspapers on the floor, drinking out of cracked mugs and sharing bags of chips. That was when Cathy went to the toilet. A few seconds later she let out this amazing scream. Andy had painted the toilet in white gloss – all of it – the seat, the handle, the bowl – everything. Cathy couldn't find the light switch and she'd sat down on the seat. She came hopping out with her tights around her knees yelling. After she'd been and cleaned herself up, she came back and started chasing Andy round the room, armed with a soggy mop.

Rog and I sat back and laughed. Later on Adam and Meg came in for an hour and so did the other vicar, Mark. I was pleased that I knew so much about painting and decorating.

The only person who was really hopeless was Andy; everything he did went wrong. He stood on Cathy's paint pot lid and started treading paint all round the room and the worst thing he did was spill a litre of brilliant white high gloss all across the floor. I opened my mouth to say that he would be a lot more useful staying at home in bed but Cathy looked daggers at me and went over to help him clear it up. Then she spent ages wiping the paint out of his hair and off his hands and out of his trousers and wherever else he'd got it; I couldn't see why she didn't just let him sort it out himself.

Fortunately, Andy didn't stay around too long. "I'll have to go home and wash my clothes," he said. "I've got to go out in them tonight."

I thought that he was joking. I couldn't imagine anybody only having one set of clothes for working in and for going out. I said cheerio but I didn't look up from my new job of measuring the walls. I'd decided to make some shelf units. After Andy spilled the paint on the floor, I measured that as well; I thought I'd bring down some vinyl floorcovering or a little square of carpet. I'd have it looking really cosy when I'd finished.

Rog had to go home early to plan out a service for Sunday so that left me and Cathy on our own. I told her my ideas about the shelf units. "My dad has a DIY shop," I said guardedly. "He always has plenty of stuff that's, you know . . . like, out-of-range. He'd give me some if I wanted."

"Was that your dad then, this morning?" Cathy asked me. "The bloke in the sports car?"

This time it was nearly my turn to spill the paint. I closed my hands round the tin and stirred it energetically.

"I didn't want him to bring me," I explained. "I was just setting off to catch the bus. I mean, I don't know why he can't just leave me alone . . . I mean, I want to be independent. You know, I want to do things on my own. I don't want them doing things for me all the time."

Cathy nodded and looked concerned. "Would you like a cup of tea?" she said.

"Thanks."

She went to put the kettle on. When she came back, she left the painting and sat down. "Why don't you leave home?" she asked me.

I finished what I was doing, wiped my brush and stood it in some turps. Then I sat opposite Cathy on a piece of newspaper. I told her about the business and my parents' plans for me. Cathy sat and listened; when the kettle boiled, she made me a mug of tea.

When I'd finished she stared down at her mug of tea. "My mum and dad were like that," she said. "They weren't trendy and modern. But they owned a business that they wanted me to work in when I left school. The only thing I wanted to do was Art."

I nodded sympathetically as I sat and sipped my tea.

"I didn't want to disappoint them. I told them I wanted to try and get a job as a designer . . . I thought I could always go back and work in the family business if I wanted to."

I nodded. It was good to feel that Cathy had been through something similar to me. We went on talking together and I felt very warm towards her. She'd had the courage to do something that I hadn't, but knowing that she'd come out OK gave me a bit more confidence.

I went home on the bus feeling more optimistic. I was pleased I was getting on well with Cathy. I didn't want to raise my hopes too high but it would be good to have a girlfriend that I had so much in common with. She did seem to like me quite a lot, although I wondered whether she might think I was a bit conservative – sort of traditional. I don't go in for freakish clothes and hairstyles. Perhaps I ought to try, I thought. Maybe I ought to have my hair dyed or have my ears pierced. I'd have to give it some thought. I'd decided as well not to have any more painful silences with my father. Within the next two days, I told myself, I would tell him my plans for leaving home.

For reasons I found difficult to understand, it was becoming harder and harder to talk to my mum and dad. I felt as though they had a fixed idea about who I was; they had this photograph in their minds of the kind of son they'd always wanted and it never once occurred to them that the trendy young man in the picture wasn't me. That was partly my fault as well; my fault for dressing up and playing the role of a person who never existed. One morning, for instance, I went out and bought a crucifix. When I came home I tucked it inside my T-shirt. I wasn't ashamed of it. I just knew they wouldn't understand.

Another thing was that I felt unable to tell them when I started going to church. I intended mentioning it but then I kept putting it off. I went to the Anglican church with the graveyard where they'd held the funeral service for Rob. I suppose I chose that one because I'd been inside it before and so it seemed familiar.

In some ways it was disappointing. The congregation were elderly apart from a couple with two little toddlers dressed in sailor suits and shorts who looked like refugees from The Good Ship Lollipop. We had a hymn called "Fight the Good Fight" which I found pretty revolting as I'm virtually a pacifist. When I joined in the hymns my deep bass voice sounded embarrassingly loud and I felt even more stupid towards the end of the third hymn when I looked around and there was this guy standing next to me with a collection plate in his outstretched hand. I took out my wallet intending to make a generous contribution and then found to my horror that all I had with me was American Express. The old guy dropped his happy expectant smile as I tried to mime to him how I'd make it up the next time that I came.

I think the most difficult thing I've ever had to do was telling my parents I'd decided to leave home. Not only that, but that I'd decided to turn down the job they'd got lined up for me as a trainee director in *The Joint*. I thought of all the nice things my parents had done for me: the way my mum had looked after me when I was ill and all the time my dad had spent assembling storage units for my bedroom. I thought of some of the things I'd done for them as well – the time I'd spent on the computer program for the shop and all the silly cards and little presents I'd made for both of them. I didn't want to wipe that out. I didn't want them to reject me and I didn't want them to think I'd rejected them; I just wanted them to understand.

I decided to talk to my father on Sunday.

I got up and went to church. During the service, I said my own prayer. I said it during the part where the vicar prayed for the queen and all the world's rulers that they might learn to govern wisely. As people must have been praying for that for centuries and it had never made any difference, I thought it was rather a waste of time.

I knelt and rested my head on my hands and said quietly, "Please give me the courage to say what's on my mind and let me say it without hurting them." I thought that might be asking for the impossible but there seemed no harm in trying.

After lunch my dad filtered himself some coffee and settled in the living room with the Sunday Business Section. I left him alone for ten minutes, then I made myself a cup of coffee. I took it into the living room and pulled up a stool in front of him. "Have you got a few minutes?" I asked him. "I wanted to have a chat."

My father folded up his paper and laid it on the coffee table. "What's on your mind?"

I'd planned out the first part of the conversation but it didn't make it any easier. "I've been thinking things over," I said.

"Mmmm?"

"I feel as though this is quite an important sort of stage for me at the moment – leaving school, starting a new job . . . taking on responsibilities."

He nodded slowly as he sipped his coffee.

"I feel as though I need to, you know . . . find out where I'm at." I paused. I was trying to express myself in the kind of language he would understand. "I thought it might do me good to get away, to do something different for a while. I mean, if I'm working in the shop, I can't just go off and do my own thing." I hesitated. "I thought it might be best to do that now – to do it first . . . then, when I've sorted myself out I mean, I could put more energy and commitment into the business or . . . " I hesitated again. "I mean, I might feel as though I don't want to do that. I might feel as though I want to do . . . something else."

My father stood up, walked over to the cocktail bar and poured himself a Jack Daniels. He spent a long time scooping out ice to go with it. "Would you like a drink?" he asked me.

I was going to say no, because I felt OK with the coffee but I decided to let him pour me one. "Thanks. I'll have a rum and Coke," I said.

He came back with the drinks and sat down again. He was opening his mouth to speak but I thought I'd say my piece first. "I don't want you to think I'm not grateful," I said. "I mean I am grateful . . . for everything you've done for me. I mean, you've been really great and . . . I mean, the business is fantastic, it's just that . . . I need to find out where I'm at just now."

He looked at me in a strange way, almost as if he'd never noticed me before. I felt that he was trying to read my thoughts, trying to pick up clues about what I was really thinking. He was realizing as well, I think, that he didn't know me well enough to do that. I don't think he knew me at all.

"It doesn't sound a bad idea," he said. "It would be good for you to travel – see the world a bit. I mean, I have . . . I *had* been rather relying on your helping out in the shop, but . . . well, if you've got things you want to do, take a few weeks off say and then . . . let's fix it say for October, say you'll start in the shop in October."

I didn't say anything.

"Or even . . . I mean, if you want a real break, leave it till nearer Christmas. Just come in in time to help us with the Christmas rush."

I sighed. I didn't know what to say.

"Have you decided, I mean . . . have you thought about where you want to go?" My dad looked a bit more enthusiastic. "You could go on a kibbutz, couldn't you? Have you thought about that? One of my mates did that in the sixties. Or go over to the States, eh? Travel about a bit. *On the Road*." His face began to look quite animated and I could tell he was starting already to plan my trip out for me – the trip he'd always wanted to take and had never found time to manage.

I didn't know how to tell him that I didn't want to be Jack Kerouac or the hippy guy in *Zen and the Art of Motor Cycle Maintenance*. All I wanted was to be me.

I drank my rum and Coke and tried to explain to him about the inner city project. When I mentioned the Fellowship, I stressed the word *Radical*. I gave the Christian bit a miss. That was something he wouldn't understand.

I told him that I wanted to leave home and live in the inner city where the project was. I wanted to live in a bedsit and see if I could manage on the kind of money that most people had to live on. That was the difficult thing. I knew they couldn't contemplate my leaving home without taking any money. I'd been thinking about that. I didn't know if I could get a job when there was so much unemployment; I wanted to be independent but it didn't seem right to live off the dole when there was money available for me if I wasn't too proud to accept it.

I finally convinced my father that I didn't know how long it would take me to find myself as we put it, but six weeks probably wasn't long enough. The time-gap before I became a trainee director in the firm would have to be left indefinite. Privately, I thought of giving it fifty years.

M E M O R A N D U M

23 July, 1985

To: The Home Office

From: Special Branch
Scotland Yard

Subject: SB/99821/RVCR77/110/462

Permission requested for addition to warrant no: SB/CND/4510/110 in respect of subject, National CRO no: SB/99821/RVCR77/110/462.

Subject has been a member of the Young Communist League and the Campaign for Nuclear Disarmament. Also, Greenpeace supporter and member of Friends of the Earth.

Members of his family are known subversives and Trotskyists.

Subject is an active member of the Radical Christian Fellowship.

The arrangement that we came to was that my parents would give me an allowance of a bit more than I'd get on the dole. I'd give this up if I found a job. They also insisted on me keeping my American Express. "What if you had an emergency?" my mother said. "What if you were stranded at an airport? Or if you bought a meal in a restaurant and found you couldn't pay?" I didn't think that was very likely. I didn't think I'd be visiting many airports or restaurants in the future, but I agreed to keep my charge card for the family account just to save them worrying.

The first thing was to find somewhere to live. I spent some time in Rothwell – where the project was – looking round at adverts in shop windows for bedsitters and flats.

I tied that in with working on the new centre. I visited *The Joint* and strolled about the store-room picking out items with damaged packets, earmarked for the January sale. I found some off-cuts of wood for shelving, an assortment of carpet squares left over from last year's range and some pieces of flooring vinyl to lay on the rest of the floor.

I loaded a trolley and walked up and down the aisles. The store-room was vast, like an aeroplane hangar, with a high vaulted roof. My footsteps echoed when I walked and when I stopped, everything was still. The shop was next door. In the distance I could hear piped music, messages on the tannoy and the bleeping of the cash tills, but all of it seemed a long way off. In the store-room it was silent. I stood still, breathing the scent of the freshly-sawn timber. It reminded me of the store-room in the little shop my father had when I was small. I remembered helping him to cut the wood, and to stack it on the floor. The little shop was a world and a half away now, but the smell of the wood was the same. I thought I might miss that.

I remembered when I was six or seven and I'd only just learned to read, I tried to make out the wording on the letter-heads and on the bills. My father spelled out the letters for me: J–o C–h–r–i–s–t–o–p–h–e–r D.I.Y. Then he took me outside and showed me the nameplate over the door and asked me to try and read it. It said the same. "In another twelve years," he said to me, "I'll have that nameplate changed." He wrote down what the new nameplate would say and asked me to try and read it:

Jo Christopher and Son.

I collected my stuff together and went to dispatch and asked them to deliver it; I knew they'd have to make a special journey. Rothwell didn't feature on *The Joint*'s delivery list.

Two days later, I went to Rothwell and walked round the post offices and newsagents, collecting phone numbers and addresses of rooms to rent. Most of them were pretty depressing. I didn't realize that people lived in places without bathrooms or hot water. I started to make a mental list of what my basic requirements were: I wanted a bath or a shower, a kitchen that I didn't have to share and, if the place looked really filthy and grotty, a landlord who didn't mind me painting it.

That turned out to be too much to ask. I spent a really depressing time looking round all the addresses on my list. Some of them were horrific. One landlord showed me a room, smaller than our bathroom, with a whole family living there. Other places had fungus growing on the walls, they had wallpaper peeling off with damp and smelled of dry rot, blocked drains and centuries of dirt and grease. If my mother had seen them, she'd have been sick.

The last room that I looked at was the one I liked the best, but even so, it was pretty bad. It was an attic with a sloping ceiling and a view across the city; that was what I liked about it. The bad points were that it was only one room; it needed painting, decorating and swilling out with disinfectant; the bathroom downstairs was shared with five other people; there was only a pay-phone and you had to put money in a meter for the gas. I was going to turn it down but then I realized that the chances were I wouldn't find anything better. I could always give it a coat of paint before I moved in, put up some new curtains and some posters and, with a few bits of my own furniture, it might not look too bad. Mr Mohammet didn't take American Express but I went out and got some cash and paid him the first month's rent before I could change my mind.

On Sunday morning I went to the Radical Christian service feeling a lot happier. Roger invited us all to a party at his house the following Saturday and that cheered me up.

There were people at the service that I hadn't seen before. Andy brought a couple of the vegan friends he shared his house with and there was a new bloke called Jamie, who'd just moved out from London. He was a few years older than me. He had longish dishevelled hair, a beard and a moustache but he didn't look like an ageing hippy; he seemed quite nice. I talked to him about the new centre and he was very keen to help. He said he might come on the Tuesday when we intended to finish off the work.

First of all on Tuesday, I put some polyurythene on the shelves and laid the floor tiles that I'd had delivered. Jamie turned up with a couple of old index files he said we could have and we used that as an opportunity to take a break. Andy made everyone a cup of tea then walked out of the kitchen and put the teapot down straight on my wet varnish. I felt livid. I picked up the teapot and the varnish was sticking to the bottom like strands of treacle; what had been a smooth and beautiful shelf top was now a sticky tacky mess. I walked to the other side of the room and took a few deep breaths before I pointed out to Andy what he'd done. "Oh," he said and laughed.

"I'll have to varnish the shelf again," I told him.

He chuckled again.

The others laughed as well. They seemed to think it was funny. I couldn't see the joke myself. I quietly drank my tea then went straight over and varnished the shelf again.

After that I did a few other little jobs with bits and pieces that I'd brought. I fixed up a row of hooks in the kitchen to hang mugs on and some larger hooks near the outside door for people to hang their coats. I checked out the lock on the door which was really old and decrepit and I offered to bring down a burglar alarm; my father was testing out a new security system and I knew we'd have one spare in a couple of weeks' time.

I felt proud to be doing something useful. Although I was trying not to show off, I wanted people to notice what a good job I was doing. It was Cathy really that I wanted to impress. I kept saying things to her like, "What height do you think the coat hooks ought to be? I don't want to make them too high." Cathy was engrossed in a discussion with Andy about veganism, asking him what kind of meals he cooked and how he managed to work out a balanced diet. She came over and suggested the height for the coat hooks, but then she went back and talked to Andy. I just got on with my work.

Going home on the bus I started thinking about Cathy. I realized that I liked her and that we seemed to have a lot in common. The sad thing was that my other experiences with girls had put me off the prospect of getting involved again. I didn't know what to do.

I thought about Roger's party. I knew that Cathy would be there and, because Rog had said that there were plenty of mattresses and sleeping bags, the chances were that both of us would stay the night. I thought then about the possibility of going to bed with Cathy. I could see a few problems there as we'd probably be sharing a room with a dozen other people. Judging by my track record, I might find difficulties having sex with Cathy in private; performing in front of an audience would be an invitation to disaster.

I thought about her later in the evening when I was sorting out my wardrobe. I was deciding which clothes to take with me to my new flat and thinking what to wear for the party next week as well. It occurred to me that if I could talk to Cathy about the problems I had with girls, she might be really understanding and sympathetic. I imagined myself explaining to Cathy how I felt. In fact, I talked to Cathy all the time that I was sorting out my wardrobe and I felt a bit embarrassed when I suddenly realized that I was actually talking to myself.

The same thing happened the next day when I was going through my tapes. While I was trying to decide whether my father would feel hurt if I left behind all the Bruce Springsteen tracks he'd ever bought me, I found myself having this conversation with Cathy. "What I think's really positive about me," I told her, "is that I'm just not into *scoring*. I mean, I know lots of blokes that are and . . . well, I mean, actually, I really despise that, I mean, that's just treating women as sex objects."

I imagined Cathy nodding her head in approval.

"I mean, what I think is really important," I told her, "is communication. I mean, I think the most important thing is to be able to really talk to somebody. Getting to know somebody on that . . . on that deeper sort of level . . . to me that's a lot more important than sex."

I decided that my father might not be so offended at my leaving behind all the tapes he'd ever bought me if I told him I knew they'd be safer at home than in my flat. I started to unpack Dire Straits and the Rolling Stones.

"What I feel," I confided in Cathy, "is that . . . well, sometimes I think there can be too much pressure to get into physical relationships. I mean, well, sex is OK, I mean, it's a very beautiful experience but, as far as I'm concerned, I think it's probably better for people to have that . . . well, that kind of relationship where they really trust each other."

As I replaced The Pogues and Billy Bragg, I imagined Cathy putting her arms round me and hugging me. "That's great," she said warmly. "You know, I'm starting to feel quite fond of you."

I put my arms round her and kissed her.

MEMORANDUM

Date: 30 July 1985

To: Equipment Development Division
PO Operational Programming Department
OP5
93 Bury Road
London

From: J. Patterson

Reference: JC110

Subject: SB/99821/RVCR77/110/462

I enclose Home Office Warrant No: SB/CND45/49960 relating to 7, Windermere Road, Bishopston. Telephone no: 0842 982761.

The enclosed list of telephone numbers are the connections we wish you to log. Transcripts should be hand delivered at the end of the calendar month unless you receive any other instructions from this office. National CRO no: SB/99821/RVCR77/110/462.

Subject has been a member of the Young Communist League and the Campaign for Nuclear Disarmament. Also, Greenpeace supporter and member of Friends of the Earth.

Members of his family are known subversives and Trotskyists.

Subject is an active member of the Radical Christian Fellowship.

I give my report. I exude efficiency. Well-trimmed fingernails, polished shoes. Everything shows attention to detail because everything counts in this job. They're watching you all the time.

There's a silence. No. In my head the words keep screaming out, pulsing with an intensity so loud that I can hardly believe he doesn't hear them. *I do not want this job*, my thoughts shout out. *I hate it. I want to wash my hands of the whole affair.*

"What's your assessment of the subject?" he asks me.

I lean forward to look eager and clear my throat to give me time to think. "I, er, agree with your assessment . . . " I start off, "insofar as the . . . er . . . potential . . . "

He nods with approval. Why do I have to say that? Why do I have to play his stupid games?

The Boss smiles at me benignly – like my teachers when I took them the homework list. The smile that says: *Good boy.* Pat, pat. *Good boy.* Stroke, stroke. They throw the stick and you rush away, searching, scrummaging through the brush. You find the stick and you race back, panting, tail wagging, ears straight back. *Good dog.* Pat, pat. *Good dog.* Stroke, stroke. *Who's a clever boy, then . . . ?*

"Well, you've done a very good job, so far." He pats my beautifully presented folder. "We're very pleased with you."

I smile with his approval. He can trust in me; he relies on me to do a good job. Pat, pat. Stroke, stroke. The words in my head are there, but quieter now. They've faded into the background. I try to remember what they said. The route is blocked by the pleasure of success.

"Have you lost your reservations about the subversive nature of this . . . er . . . subject?"

People are never called people in this job. Everyone has to be dehumanized. But he's reminded me. There was something I wanted to tell him. I try to remember what I said before. Potential – that was the let-out clause. That was the word that helped me say two things at once.

"I can see what you mean about him having the potential," I start off. "I mean, his family, his . . . associates. I just feel at the moment as though he's . . . " I somehow can't bring myself to say the word, innocent. "Well, he seems more suited to being a Sunday School teacher than a spy."

He smiles at me and nods.

"You know we're not looking for spies," he corrects me. "Subversives."

"Well, I didn't mean . . . "

"As Lord Harris said in 1978, 'subversives can be described as those who threaten the safety and well-being of the state by political, industrial or violent means.' And, of course, any adverse public reaction to government policies can be legitimately considered as a threat to security."

This is totally ridiculous. I can't think what to say.

"We must never underestimate the intelligence of the subjects we're dealing with. Most of them, as you well know, are gullible idealists." He smiles condescendingly. "That doesn't exonerate them, of course. Those sort of individuals can be easily led, but . . . just supposing . . . supposing we had someone very clever . . . I mean, what is it that makes you think that this young man is so innocent?"

I stare at his desk as I stroke my beard and try to look as if I'm thinking. "Well, I've got most of my information from his diary. He just comes over as a very well-meaning Christian."

"And if these subversives were a little cleverer than we think . . . isn't that the sort of red herring that they'd plant for us to pick up?"

I think he's paranoid. I think that most of the people in this organization are completely paranoid. They can't trust anyone. They may recruit paranoid people to join the organization or it may be that working here makes them like that. I'm not sure.

I nod my head in resignation. "I suppose so."

"We always have to be several steps ahead. Remember that."

He probably makes his wife eat everything first in case

it's poisoned. He might even have the house replastered every year to search for secret listening devices hidden behind the wallpaper.

"We're very pleased with the work you're doing. You'll go a long way."

I wag my tail and straighten back my ears. Stroke, stroke. Pat, pat. *Who's a clever boy, then . . . ?*

"I'm pleased to be able to help," I tell him, lying through my teeth.

* * *

The kitchen was filled with people, talking together and laughing; in the next room Dire Straits were singing "Walk of Life"; the air was heavy with dope and with the smell of home-brewed beer, vegan-style pizzas, soya spring rolls and potatoes in their jackets. The shaggy dog had uncurled itself from the fireside and was bouncing round the floor snaffling up pieces of pizza.

I found Cathy in the next room talking to Andy. She was wearing a pair of men's stripy pyjamas, pink leg-warmers, high-heeled boots, several necklaces, three pairs of ear-rings and a polka dot tie. Andy was wearing the jeans he'd spilled the paint on. I hung around, thinking they hadn't seen me. It was difficult to join in the conversation because the music was so loud but when neither Andy nor Cathy spoke to me I decided to interrupt. "You never got the paint off, then . . . ?" I commented, looking at Andy's jeans.

"Sorry . . . ?"

"Your jeans . . . " I pointed.

"You what?" He looked at me vacantly.

I pointed again at the paint. He obviously couldn't hear a word I said. He leaned across and put his ear right next to my mouth. I felt stupid then, because "I see you couldn't get the paint off your jeans," isn't the kind of remark you shout into somebody's earhole. It was just something casual to say because I couldn't think of anything else. I took a deep breath and yelled, "I see you couldn't get the paint off your jeans!"

He looked really puzzled and shook his head.

"Forget it," I told him.

"You what?"

"Forget it."

"What did you say?"

There was something about Andy that always exasperated me. I shook my head and waved my hands in a "Wipe-it-out" signal. He looked as puzzled as if I'd just escaped from a lunatic asylum. I sighed deeply then went to look at the records. I was chewing on a piece of frizzled pizza which had something orange and flaky on the top that tasted of sardines. I looked at it for the first time. It occurred to me that the topping probably was a powdered sardine. But what were the yellow flecks?

I squeezed my way past a crowd of fifty people to go back to the kitchen and find a rubbish bin. The kitchen was even more crowded. There didn't seem to be a bin so I left my pizza on a cardboard plate containing half a baked potato, a splodge of coleslaw and a cigarette end, and looked for something to drink. What I really fancied was some fruit juice. I surveyed the assortment of bottles and cans and saw some cloudy orange liquid with lots of bits in. I decided that must be the fresh orange juice. I poured myself a drink and nearly choked. It was home-brew. Foggy home-brew with bits floating round like warm marmalade. The route to the sink was blocked by about seventy other people that I'd never seen before, but I started edging my way through.

On the way to the sink I passed Roger. "Hi, Julian," he said.

"Hi," I said, "Great party, Rog." But already I wasn't so sure.

I discreetly poured the home-brew down the sink, found myself a paper cup and set off on the great squeeze back to the table with the drinks. On the way I passed a bloke eating from a paper plate containing half a baked potato, a lump of coleslaw and the remains of my powdered sardine pizza. I couldn't see what he'd done with the cigarette end.

Cathy was now standing by the table. "Hello there," she said to me. "Are you all right?"

"Yes thanks."

"Great party, isn't it?"

"Yeah." But when I noticed that Andy was still hovering by Cathy's side, I felt even less certain. Things weren't going quite the way I'd planned.

I struggled to think of some witty remark to start up a conversation with Cathy but Andy got in first. "Do you know," he said, "that ninety per cent of British farmland is taken up with grazing and foodstuff production?"

"No," she said.

"Yes, there are 450 million farm animals slaughtered every year."

"Every year?"

"That's right. And there are 40 million hens confined in battery cages."

There was silence for a few seconds as both of them contemplated the slaughtered animals and the battery hens.

"The centre's looking really good, isn't it?" I interrupted. "The shelves look all right now," I reassured Andy. "Now I've put the other coat of varnish on. You can hardly tell it got messed up."

Andy and Cathy both nodded but neither of them looked enthusiastic.

"You see," Andy went on, "there are millions of people starving to death in countries where the farming land is used to grow animal feed. If everyone lived on vegetables there'd be plenty of food to go round."

I nodded appreciatively but I couldn't think of anything to add.

Fortunately, I noticed Jamie shoving his way through. I decided to go across and speak to him.

I was pleased I had because Jamie knew hardly anybody there. He poured himself a drink and talked to me for quite a while about the centre. "Those shelves you put up were very good," he said. "You seem to have a knack for joinery."

I was pleased he'd noticed. I told him that I'd had a lot of practice because my father owned a DIY shop. "Oh yes," he said, "that's right. You mentioned it when you talked about the burglar alarm."

Jamie said that he'd once worked for a security firm so we talked a bit about different kinds of devices and alarms; he asked me which ones we were trying out and he seemed to know a lot about it. He was quite an interesting bloke to talk to but my attention was constantly distracted by watching the progress of the relationship between Cathy and Andy in the corner.

I found it really surprising. I knew that Cathy'd been spending a lot of time with Andy but I thought that was because she felt sorry for him; it had never occurred to me that she fancied him. I couldn't work out what she saw in him. I mean, he was useless; absolutely hopeless. What made it worse was that she seemed to prefer Andy to me; that must mean that I was even more hopeless than Andy. I found that quite upsetting.

"Can I get you a drink?" Jamie asked.

I felt as though I needed one. "Is there any rum and Coke?"

"You'd be lucky. There's some wine – cheap white wine . . . "

"That'll do."

Jamie handed me a glass. "Thanks," I said. I glanced across at Cathy who now had her arm round Andy's waist. She was moving her hand down slowly towards the top of his thigh.

Jamie must have noticed where I was looking. He shook his head and grinned at me. He said in a low voice, "It takes all sorts, doesn't it? I don't know what he sees in her."

At first I felt offended, as if Jamie had insulted my girlfriend. Then I remembered that Cathy wasn't my girlfriend. And she did look a bit ridiculous. The stripy pyjamas might have seemed chic on a girl who was slim; on Cathy they just looked silly. I joined in with Jamie in grinning at them both and poured myself another glass of wine.

I was determined to have a good time. I drank too much, I danced exuberantly to all the Bruce Springsteen records and then I started telling Jamie in a loud voice all about Andy's misadventures with the paintwork at the centre. He doubled up when I told the story about Cathy sitting on the toilet with the wet paint on the seat.

I drank several glasses of wine and, when that ran out, I

started on the home-brew. I think I was wanting to get drunk. Cathy and Andy were snogging in the corner and I was trying to ignore them, but I did feel upset when I saw them leaving arm in arm. Getting drunk helped me feel OK. When it got to the early hours though, and everyone started leaving, I found myself panicking a bit. I knew that the next morning, I'd not only feel depressed, but I'd have a terrible hangover as well.

Rog organized mattresses and blankets for those of us who were staying. He wanted to go to bed because he had a service to take in the morning. Jamie said he'd just have another drink and then he'd get off. I said good night to him then staggered upstairs to crash out on my mattress.

I realized I'd got problems when I tried to find the handle to the bedroom door. I found myself groping the wall at the other end of the landing facing in the wrong direction. Turning myself round and walking towards the bedroom took an amazing effort of will. I found my bedroom but once I got inside, the walls started slowly spinning and I didn't know whether I was going to fall unconscious or be sick. Just in case, I thought I'd better stagger to the toilet. I felt dreadful. I could hardly walk. I went into the toilet, shut the door and sat down on the floor. I put my head on the floor for a moment and the next thing I heard was the sound of people banging on the door. I must have blacked out. I crawled across and opened the door and sat outside on the landing while I tried to remember where I was.

I decided I would have to make a mega-effort to get to bed when I had an unpleasant thought: I'd left my jacket downstairs in the hall. There had been hundreds of people at the party, most of whom I didn't know. It was daft to leave my best jacket in the hall with my wallet, my American Express and my house keys in the pocket. It seemed a stupid thing to do in the state I was in but I decided to stagger downstairs and look for it.

There weren't all that many coats and jackets left in the hall, but those that were kept spinning and swaying as if they were on a merry-go-round. When I leant across to grab a leather jacket, it shifted away all by itself and left me slithering down the wall like a misthrown jelly. Then I thought I could see my jacket, on the bottom hook near the door, but when I leaned forward again, it vanished and changed into a yucca plant. I tried to bring my brain into focus. Which jacket had I been wearing? Had I worn a jacket at all? Or had I been wearing a yucca plant? Whose house was I in? Where was I? Who was I? And who was the yucca plant?

I knew I was going to pass out again. I tottered into the kitchen to see if Jamie was still there, but there was no one left. Then I looked in the living room. There were only two people, groping on the settee. I decided to lie down on the floor for a few moments while I gathered my energy to make it back upstairs.

That was the last thing I remembered.

The next morning I felt terrible, absolutely dreadful. I'd been dreaming I was in an aeroplane that had gone out of control, dipping and diving through the clouds. I was still conscious of the roar of its damaged engine when I woke up and found Rog gently shaking me. The plane engine was the droning of the hoover.

"I've brought you some coffee," he said.

"Thanks." I struggled to remember where I was. I tried to raise myself up but the sudden movement caused a pain like a road drill tearing through my skull. I groaned. "My head . . ."

"Have you got a hangover?"

I nodded weakly from my shoulders, moving my head as little as possible.

"I'll get you some aspirins," said Rog. "Try and drink your coffee."

I reached for the mug that he was holding out. Then the room started spinning and I sank back to the floor.

"Here, look," said Rog. "I'll put your coffee down here." He seemed concerned about me. "You try and drink it. I'll go and get you something for your headache."

He left. I was pleased to have a reprieve while I just lay still and did nothing.

I knew I was at Roger's. I knew there had been a party. But all that I remembered was the picture of Cathy and Andy setting off home with their arms around each other. I closed my eyes and wondered if this could be part of the bad dream along with the crashing aircraft. It wasn't. I prised myself on to my elbow and started sipping at my coffee.

"I've brought you some paracetamol." This time it was Jamie standing over me. "I've just called in to help tidy up. Rog said you weren't looking too good."

When I made no move to take the tablets, Jamie shook two out of the drum and passed them to me.

"Thanks."

"You shouldn't have mixed your drinks," he told me.

I didn't remember mixing any drinks. I didn't remember anything. I just wanted to go back to sleep.

"You're the last one to get up," said Jamie. "You ought to try and make a move. Can't you sleep it off when you get home?"

I nodded feebly.

"Look, you get up slowly while I finish clearing up the mess in the kitchen. Then I'll give you a lift home. You're in no state to go back on your own."

"It's OK," I told him. "I'll be all right."

He shook his head. "Come on, I'll take you back."

There were lots of reasons why I didn't want Jamie to take me home, but I couldn't remember what they were. I just nodded, as slowly as I could.

Later, sitting in Jamie's Metro, struggling to stop myself from heaving up whenever we went round a corner, I managed to remember that I was living with my parents still and I wasn't too keen on people seeing where that was. Jamie kept asking me for directions and I did think about asking him to drop me somewhere else and catching the bus the rest of the way but, for one thing, there were hardly any buses on a Sunday and, for another, I knew I might spew up at any minute. I just felt really thankful that he was there to take me home.

"Would you like to come in and have a cup of coffee?" I said as we pulled up at the bottom of the drive.

"No thanks. I've got things I need to do. Some other time . . ."

"Well, it's really good of you. I don't know how I'd have got back on my own."

"Anytime," he said. "I should go straight to bed and sleep it off."

I nodded. "See you."

"Cheers."

I staggered out of the car and up the drive.

I didn't get to bed for several hours. When I walked into the house there was a strange man in the kitchen, peering closely at the window ledge. We'd had burglars yet again.

My parents couldn't believe it. "What happened to the burglar alarm?" I asked my mum. "Wasn't it switched on?"

She shook her head. "We just can't understand it," she said. "It was working perfectly. The amazing thing is that it's just like the last time – they don't seem to have taken anything."

The detective was waiting to interview me. He asked me first of all how old I was, then asked whether I wanted my parents present. I thought that seemed a funny thing to ask and I told him that I'd rather answer questions on my own. Once the interview started I understood why he thought I might want to have my parents with me: it seemed as though I was the number one suspect.

He wanted to know everything about the night before: where I'd slept, who I'd been with and a list of people who could corroborate my story. I felt really angry. Why would I want to rob my parents? They gave me everything I wanted. In the end, I told him what I thought. "This is stupid," I said. "You're wasting time interviewing me. You'd be better looking for fingerprints and stuff."

He paused. "Most crimes are committed by people who know the victims well," he explained. "We always start closest to home."

It seemed ages before he went. By the time he left, my stomach was churning like the inside of an automatic washer. I couldn't tell if I was about to be sick, have a fit of diarrhoea or both at once. When I did stagger into the lavatory I didn't know whether to sit on it, stand in front of it or kneel over it. And trying to do all three at once didn't do my vertigo much good.

What made it worse was the pain searing through my skull. The effects of the paracetamol were wearing off. I fumbled with the catch on the bathroom cabinet, found some more tablets and swallowed a couple. Then I staggered into my bedroom and crashed out on the duvet.

The room started swirling in every direction like a Waltzer at the fair. I hoped I wouldn't be sick – not before I woke up, anyway. Lying there, helpless, I remembered Cathy. I remembered the look in her eyes as she talked to Andy; I remembered the movement of her hand round Andy's waist, round his hips, down towards his thighs. The picture seared my soul like the pain pulsing through my skull. And I felt too ill to cry.

I had another thought in the half-moment before sleep: the first job I should do when I woke up was check that my new diary was still there.

Ministry of Defence
Main Building
Whitehall
LONDON SW1A 2H8

"D" Notices on British Intelligence Services
and Ciphers and Communications

PRIVATE AND CONFIDENTIAL

File JC 110
Part III

RIVELIN VALLEY CRIMINAL RECORDS

INPUT DATE:	20/09/85	**SEX:**	Male
SURNAME:	Christopher	**FORENAME(S):**	Julian
NICKNAME(S):	none known	**ALIAS(ES):**	none known
P.O.B:	Maidstone	**D.O.B:**	25/12/66

ADDRESS: 7 ("Highgrass"), Windermere Road, Bishopston

STREET TYPE: Upper class suburbia

ABOVE ADDRESS VERIFIED: 01/09/85

VEHICLE(S): none

HEIGHT:	5ft 7ins	**PHOTO NO:**	SB/110/3/27/84
EYE COLOUR:	blue	**BUILD:**	slim
RACE:	white	**HAIR:**	brown
FACIAL HAIR:	none	**ABNORMALITIES:**	none

RIVELIN VALLEY CRO NO: 347/84/110

SECURITY LEVEL: Special Branch

REASON(S) FOR INTEREST: Membership of subversive organizations, parents under surveillance

LAST CONVICTION DATE: no convictions

REMARKS:
Membership of Young Communist League from 08/11/80
Membership of Campaign for Nuclear Disarmament (Rivelin Valley Youth Branch) from 28/01/81
Friends of the Earth membership from 18/03/70 (Family membership)
Greenpeace supporter (Family subscription) 01/09/84)
Sighted: Youth CND stall, Bishopston precinct, 16/03/85 and 07/04/85
Radical Christian Fellowship, June 1985

MYSTERY BREAK-IN AT HOME OF DIY BOSS.

Local businessman, Jo Christopher, told the Rivelin Valley Chronicle today why he was "incredulous" to find that thieves had broken into the family's luxury home in the prestigious Windermere Valley development.

Said Mr Christopher today, "We were just testing out a new high-security burglar alarm system for the shop. It's incredible that anyone should have found a way through it and, even more unthinkable that, having found a way into the house, they stole nothing at all."

The mystery break-in is still baffling the local C.I.D. Valuable cameras and stereo equipment in the luxury home were left untouched, as were a video, jewellery belonging to Mrs Christopher and many other items of value.

Said Mr Christopher, "Like most of the families in the area, we've got plenty of stuff to interest a thief. It's just amazing that anyone should go to so much trouble to enter the house, examine all our personal files and papers and then just leave everything behind."

Police want to interview anyone who was in the Windermere Road area between 8 and 11pm on Saturday evening.

Flat 15
St Hilda's Walk
Olive Mount Avenue
Bishopston

23 Sept 1985

Daytoday Diaries
Printpoint House
London Road
Swansea

Dear Sirs

I had one of your diaries bought me last year for a Christmas present. I have not been using the diary for the last few months and now find, sadly, that I have lost the key.

It would be a shame to spoil such a nice diary by breaking the lock and I wondered whether you would be kind enough to send a replacement key.

I enclose a postal order for £2.50 to cover the cost of the key and the postage and to compensate you for the trouble.

Yours faithfully

J Patterson

Mr J. Patterson

Mr. J. Patterson
Flat 15
St Hilda's Walk
Olive Mount Avenue
Bishopston

28th September, 1985

Dear Mr Patterson,

Thank you for your letter. We have pleasure in enclosing another key for your diary, plus a spare in case you should ever lose it again.

We are also enclosing a catalogue of our products for next season, all of which are available by mail order from the above address.

We are pleased that you have found our products useful.

Yours sincerely,

G. Sharp

Mr. G. Sharp
Sales Manager

PRINTPOINT HOUSE, LONDON ROAD, SWANSEA

I didn't wake up until quite late in the evening. I staggered downstairs to make myself a cup of coffee and then I remembered again about the diary. While the coffee was filtering I went upstairs to look for it. Normally I keep it on the shelf at the back of my storage unit behind my portable TV. It wasn't there. I searched around the shelves, taking out books and files and then replacing them. The diary had definitely gone.

I went downstairs and collected my coffee and wondered what to do. I knew I ought to tell somebody but it seemed so stupid. Why should anyone want to steal my diary? I couldn't understand it.

As I was thinking what to do, the phone rang. It was Rog. "Hi, Jules," he said. "I just thought I'd phone and see how you were."

"I'm fine."

"You didn't look so good this morning."

"Well, I feel better now I've slept it off. Look, I'm sorry, I mean, I did intend to stay behind and help tidy up."

"Oh, that's OK. It only took us an hour or so."

"It was stupid of me to get so drunk."

"Well, everybody does it once in a while."

I told Rog then about the burglary. He was really shocked when I told him how the detective seemed to look on me as a suspect.

"That's ridiculous," he said. "You weren't in a fit state to find your way upstairs to your bedroom last night, let alone out to Windermere Road and back."

"I know. It's just ridiculous."

"Haven't you told them?"

"Yes. But they say they want witnesses and everything."

"That's ridiculous. Look, I'll call in at the police station. I'll tell them I was with you last night and that I woke you up this morning and you were in no fit state for playing burglars."

"I don't want to put you to any trouble."

"That's no trouble. It'll only take ten minutes."

I felt really pleased about that. I thought about telling Rog about the diary, but I decided not to. I thought I'd better have another search round first. I could have put it somewhere else.

Later in the week, after I'd moved into my flat, I went out for a drink with Jamie. We'd been working together at the centre and then decided to go over to The Crown – a really old-fashioned little pub just down the road. We sat in the snug next to the coal fire surrounded by an assortment of old-age pensioners playing dominoes and a group of women having a silly night out together. The juke box was playing, the fruit machine was whirring, the dominoes were clattering and the women kept erupting into fits of laughter. It was really warm and friendly.

We talked about the centre and how well it was coming on, and we talked about my flat. Then Jamie said he thought I'd been looking a bit depressed and asked if there was anything on my mind. I felt a bit taken aback. "It's not much of a Christian Fellowship if you can't talk about your problems, is it?" Jamie said.

That seemed true enough. I nibbled on my crisps and drank my beer while I thought about what to say. I felt stupid telling him about Cathy after he'd made fun of her at the party, but it made me feel good to think there was somebody that I could share my problems with.

The difficulty was that I didn't know where to start. I felt embarrassed telling another bloke that I had problems with sex but the good thing about Jamie was that he seemed to sense that. "I'd guess it's either problems with your parents or with a girl," he said.

I nodded.

"They're both disaster areas."

We grinned at each other.

"Come on, let me buy you another drink."

When Jamie came back from the bar, I started explaining to him about Cathy. He seemed really sympathetic, so I also told him about Kerry Ann and even my misadventure with Clare. He seemed concerned, especially when I mentioned about my father buying me the contraceptives.

"That bloke's got a lot to answer for," he said.

"He means well."

Jamie shook his head and drank his lager.

"You know," he said, "when you talked about Cathy, you said you were hoping to make a good impression on her . . . like, you know, with the jobs you were doing at the centre . . . "

"Mmmmm."

"Well, the things you were doing – the jobs you were talking about – I mean, aren't they the kind of things you used to do to try and impress your father?"

I thought about that for a moment. "I don't know. Maybe," I said.

Jamie smiled and shook his head. "Look, it's no use trying to impress your father," he said, "when he's not around." He patted my shoulder. "You have to do what you want to do; not what your father wants. I mean, you can't spend the rest of your life trying to please somebody who isn't going to be there to see you and doesn't appreciate you anyhow."

It was hard to see the truth in that but I guessed he might be right.

We talked some more and I drank two glasses of beer but then I went on to fruit juice; I didn't want to get a hangover again. I began to warm towards Jamie; it was really helpful, just having him to talk to. There were all kinds of ways – like with the thing about my father, for instance – where he seemed to understand me really well. I'd never had a proper friend like that before; not since Rob died.

At closing time, I invited Jamie back to my flat for a coffee. It felt good to have a place of my own at last and a friend to invite back with me. He looked at the view and admired the different jobs I'd done and then we sat down on the bit of worn carpet and played some tapes and drank instant coffee.

When Jamie left it was late, time for me to go to bed. I made myself another cup of coffee and stood by the window and looked out over the city. It was a clear starlit night with a panorama of lights from the street lamps and the multi-storey blocks. It was beautifully peaceful.

I tried not to think about Cathy because, when I did, it hurt. I don't think it was because Cathy and I were made for each other and I don't think I'd fallen in love but I felt hurt just the same. If I'd had lots of other successful relationships with women, then it might not have mattered so much, but I felt sure there must be something about me that people found really off-putting. I felt a terrible sense of failure.

I stood by the window and drank my coffee and I prayed that I wouldn't start feeling sorry for myself. I didn't want things like that to get me down.

I looked out over the city and, for the first time since I'd decided to leave home, I felt an awareness of my freedom. There was no more questioning, no more wondering whether it was the right thing to do or not. I looked down at the traffic and the lights of the town below me and then I heard a loud thought in my head. It took a while for it to focus and it was hard to put it into words. I had a mission. That was the feeling that I had, that there was work for me to do.

I didn't know what the work would be, but I felt it would be important. I had a vision of somehow reaching out and speaking to other people, the people out there in the city. It was an uncanny sensation, a strange picture of myself, because it didn't seem like me at all. It seemed more like someone else.

Before I climbed into bed, I took out my Bible. I'd started to study the Old Testament prophets and I liked to read the next little bit at night before I went to sleep. Just as I was settling down, I remembered another book I needed – it's a sort of commentary that explains parts of the Bible that are difficult to understand. I started rooting through my packing cases, looking for it.

I found the book I needed, then something else caught my eye. Underneath some magazines was a little patch of blue. I recognized it straightaway. I reached down and pulled it out. I stared at it and then I shook my head. I could hardly believe I was getting so absentminded. It was my diary. The one I thought I'd lost. It must have been one of the first things I'd packed up in my box.

Early in the New Year we decided to join in a picket. It was at a local factory where women had been sacked for trying to join a trade union. A group of us drove out in Jamie's car – Jamie, Rog, Meg and myself – a couple of others were coming on the bus. Jamie parked the Metro in the street behind the factory opposite four vanloads of policemen. As we walked past, we could see them through the windows. They were eating sandwiches, drinking tea and reading *The Sun* and *The Daily Express*.

As we approached the factory, people were strolling up and down selling the *Socialist Worker, Socialist Action, The Next Step* and *Militant*; others hurried past carrying trade union banners and placards saying, The Union Fights for Union Rights. Building up as we got nearer was the sound of chanting, shouts and jeers. It reminded me of the street behind the football ground on a Saturday afternoon.

Outside the factory gates were a couple of thousand men standing shoulder to shoulder. In front of them I could just make out a long chain of policemen. The men kept pushing and swaying, shoving their weight against the straggling blue line singing, *Here we go, Here we go, Here we go* and *Apple Sauce, Apple Sauce, Apple Sauce.*

Just then, a great jeer broke out. The crowd furthest away from us swayed forward like a wave of bodies at a football match. We could see the front line of policemen bracing themselves. The shouting and jeering grew louder and I saw the group of women walking into work.

I expected them to be arriving in a bus. There were only fifteen or twenty of them and they walked uncertainly into the empty arena. It looked as if they might get hurt. The line of policemen was nearly breaking already and there was no sign of the reinforcements who'd been eating their sandwiches in the vans.

The men around me were swearing and spitting and waving their fists in the air. I felt alienated from them. They should have been angry at whoever owned the factory, not the women who couldn't afford to stay away from work.

Behind us the crowd was building up. As the workers walked through the arena, the men thronged nearer to the side of the gates where the ranks of policemen were weaker. The jeering rose into a chant: *Scab! Scab! Scab!* Then, *Here we go; here we go; here we go* and the bodies surged forward like a torrent in a storm.

I tried to stay my ground; I tried to stay upright and I tried to hold on to Meg who was crushed between a press photographer and a man selling *Socialist Action.* I didn't want to push into anyone else but the crowd behind were shoving so hard that I started falling forward. I had to let go of Meg. I held out my arms to support myself and fell on the people in front.

The line of policemen folded with the pressure. I staggered through and Meg stumbled beside me.

Men clambered over the policemen and rushed towards the group of women.

The policeman must have come at me from behind. I didn't see him. I wasn't conscious of the blue serge uniform until an arm grabbed me by the throat. I felt shocked at the way he just screwed up my shirt in his fist. I tried to explain that all I was doing was trying to stop myself from falling but he didn't give me the chance. He punched me in the stomach. It wasn't the pain that I was aware of straightaway but the unfair and sudden force. It didn't feel like someone's hand that hit me; it was more like a battering ram. I doubled up. I tried to get my breath but it was just as if my lungs had been torn apart. I thought I was going to be sick.

I collapsed down to my knees and someone kicked me from behind. Then I saw the policeman's hand rise in the air. I looked up. He was holding a truncheon and aiming it towards my head. I tried to cry out but I was speechless. I still couldn't get my breath. I put up my hands to protect myself but the movement was strangely slow and weak as if the hands belonged to someone else.

Suddenly, there was a swift movement at my side. A hand cut sharply through the air and the policeman was on the ground. Jamie was there. He'd knocked down the policeman with some kind of karate chop. He put his arms under me and dragged me away from the crowd as I still tried to get my breath. "Are you all right?"

I nodded. I couldn't speak.

Two other policemen fell on Jamie. They lifted him by his armpits then twisted his wrists behind his back and frog-marched him away. "I'm only trying to help my mate," I heard him saying. "Look, he needs an ambulance." They took no notice.

In the chaos round me, I'd lost sight of Meg, Rog and anyone else I knew. Policemen were lashing out with truncheons, hitting at anyone in reach. The women workers were looking after themselves with an assortment of handbags and umbrellas. One of them wielded a *Read the Workers Hammer* placard like a club, beating a cowering paper seller. Someone fell on top of me. I knew I had to get away. My breath was coming in tiny spurts. I thought that maybe, if I found some corner to revive in, I might manage to stay alive.

I caught sight of Jamie standing near the road. He had his wallet open and was showing something to the group of policemen. It seemed to be some form of identification. It was probably his driving licence. One of the policemen was speaking on his radio. After a few moments he nodded at

Jamie and they let him walk away.

I was crawling out of the mêlée on my hands and knees when Jamie found me. He ran across and put his arm around my shoulders. "Are you OK?"

I nodded.

He helped me stagger towards the gate. "Here, let's have a look at you. You're bleeding."

He pointed to the bloodstains on the bottom of my shirt. I hadn't noticed them before.

"Come on, sit down here. Let's have a look."

I sat on the ground while Jamie took a freshly-folded white handkerchief out of his pocket and used it to wipe away the blood.

He wiped around the cut and graze which were just below the waistband of my jeans. "I think it's stopped bleeding now," he said. "I don't think it's very deep. But you'd better get it seen to."

He gave me the handkerchief to hold. "I'll go and fetch the car round," he said. "Just stay here till I come back."

I don't know where he thought I was likely to run off to.

Jamie wanted to run me down to the local casualty but I didn't want to go. I didn't fancy waiting there all afternoon just to be told I'd got bruises and a graze. "I'd rather go home," I said. "I'll just sit down for an hour or so–I'll be all right."

"OK. Have you got any antiseptic?"

"I don't think so."

"I'll stop and get some on the way. I'll check you over when we get back."

Jamie stopped off at a chemist's and bought some antiseptic and cottonwool then he drove me home. I didn't feel too bad sitting in the car, but walking up the stairs to my attic was sheer agony.

"Sit down and have a rest," said Jamie when we got upstairs. "I'll make a cup of tea."

I sat on the edge of the bed while Jamie put the kettle on.

"Hey, what did the policemen say to you?" I asked him. I'd been so concerned about myself that I'd forgotten that Jamie was in trouble. "Are they going to charge you?"

He shook his head. "I don't think so. I reckon I've talked my way out of it."

I couldn't understand how anyone could talk their way out of karate chopping a policeman but I felt too weak to argue.

Jamie was filling a bowl with warm water and pouring in some antiseptic. The smell took me back to something a long long time ago. I wasn't sure what it was at first. Then I remembered: when I'd been in hospital when I was very small.

Jamie tore off pieces of cottonwool and soaked them in the water. "Take your shirt off," he said. "Let's look at the damage."

At first when I went in the hospital, I felt scared. It was a huge building like a castle and I was afraid I might never come out. I was wheeled by masked men on a white trolley through a labyrinth of corridors. All I could see were lights – rows and rows of round white moons.

I took off my shirt and placed it beside me on the bed.

"Turn round."

I stood up and turned around.

"You've a couple of bruises on your shoulders," he said. He touched them gently. "They should be all right." He checked down my ribs and tested my reflexes and moved my arms about. "The rest of you seems OK. It's just this cut and graze that need seeing to."

He started turning back the waistband on my jeans, then he hesitated. "Can you just lower your jeans," he said. "Let's see how far it goes."

It would have been sensible to take my jeans off but I thought I'd feel a bit stupid, sitting in my underpants so I undid the fastening and the zip and shoved my jeans down slightly.

"Come on then. Let's bathe it. Sit on the bed."

When I woke up in the hospital I was in a cubicle with curtains round. The curtains had a pattern of elephants and giraffes. Everyone was nice to me. A young nurse came and bathed my head. She soaked cottonwool in lukewarm water which smelled of antiseptic. Her uniform was stiff and starched but, when she stood close to me, I could feel the warmth and softness of her body. I felt safe. I wanted someone to look after me. I relaxed and forgot about feeling frightened.

Jamie knelt on the floor in front of me and squeezed out the cottonwool. First of all he wiped the area round the graze, where it didn't hurt. He was very gentle and careful. "I'll just clean round about," he explained. "You don't want to get any dirt in. Tell me if it stings too much."

When I woke up there was a magic roundabout, turning and playing music by my bed. There was a big brown teddy sitting by my pillow and, when the nurse came back, she fed me with ice-cream and drinks of fizzy pop. I was sad when I had to go home.

Jamie stroked my skin gently with the cottonwool. It felt warm and relaxing. Then he rinsed the cottonwool and wiped over the area again. Then he patted my skin dry.

There was something pleasantly erotic about just placing my body at somebody else's disposal; I wanted to close my eyes and let go and let the feeling just sweep over me. It had something to do with trust. I wanted to abdicate control. There was something sensual about the way that Jamie was kneeling in such close proximity to parts of my body that people usually keep their distance from and there was something very soothing about the stroking of the cottonwool around the lower part of my body.

He threw the used cottonwool away and tore off some more to bathe the part that was injured. "This is where it starts to hurt," he smiled. "It'll sting anyway." He looked up at me. "Are you OK?"

"I'm fine."

"Just relax."

I didn't want to wince in front of Jamie so I relaxed my body and took a deep breath. The water did sting, but it didn't really hurt.

"OK?"

"Yes, that's fine."

"Just relax."

I think it was the way that Jamie kept telling me to relax that made me start feeling sexy. I think that was what triggered it off. I had this strange mixture of emotions – feelings that were totally strange and unexpected.

For a few moments I started melting. It was one of those times that you encounter in a dream, where all the taboos slink away and you can sink inside a fantasy. Where sex comes suddenly sweet and warm like a jugful of condensed milk, thick and flowing. It was taking my breath away.

I'd always assumed that having sex meant putting on a performance, doing things to girls. In most of my private fantasies though, I would lie completely passive, wanting someone else to take control, willing for someone else to play with me, taking away all my responsibility.

I started to feel embarrassed. I was getting an erection. I

didn't want Jamie to notice. My instinct was to put my hand down over my crotch and try to cover up my embarrassment but I knew that would make it worse. It would make it really obvious. It wouldn't disguise what was happening. The only thing I could do was to switch myself off.

It took several seconds actually to get rid of the erection. I did it by focusing my attention on my dirty socks lying in the corner, waiting to be washed. Unfortunately Jamie had just turned down the top of my jeans a little more and was bathing the area dangerously close to the source of my discomfort. I desperately hoped he wouldn't notice. I wanted to divert his attention somehow, but I couldn't think what to say.

"I think that'll be OK now." Jamie looked up and smiled gently at me. He put down the cottonwool and reached over for the towel. He lightly dabbed the corner of my graze. As he did so, the rest of the towel fell on top of my crotch. The touch was only very slight but, because my erection had still not quite subsided, I found that even the slightest touch made me feel sexy again.

I took the towel from him and finished drying myself. "Thanks very much," I said. "It's very good of you."

"Not at all. It's a pleasure."

I felt slightly awkward afterwards as Jamie made a cup of tea and we sat down by the gas fire. But then we started talking. Jamie asked what I thought about the picket line and we both complained about the brutality of the police.

After a while I started to relax. I still felt slightly disconcerted. I mean, I didn't even know it was possible for me to get turned on by a bloke but I decided not to let it worry me. I decided that I couldn't be a closet homosexual because nothing like that had ever happened to me before. I felt fairly confident as well that Jamie had never even noticed. If he had, I think he'd have made an excuse to go straight home. I decided that the best thing would be to just try and forget about it. I thought I'd let it pass.

A few days later, I was asked to go on the radio.

I had a phone call from Rog in the morning. "Hi, Jules. I've just had this call from Dave Delmonte on Radio Rivelin. He wants someone to go on his chat show at half-past ten and talk about the project. I can't get away from work. Are you free?"

"I wouldn't know what to say."

"What he said was that he wanted someone to come on the programme and talk about our plans to alleviate poverty in the inner city."

"That sounds all right."

"And the ideas we had for raising money for the famine victims in Eritrea.

"You'd only be on for five minutes . . . you might be able to get people to send some money in."

"Mmmm." I hesitated. "I've never done anything like that before though."

"It'd be great if you could. I mean, they might not ask us again if we turn it down."

They might not ask us again if I messed it up, but I tried my best to sound confident. "OK." I said. "I'll have a go."

"Thanks, Jules. I'm sure you'll be really good."

I didn't feel so sure myself. I put the phone down, grabbed a notebook and pencil and dashed out for the bus.

Radio Rivelin was in a large converted house on the edge of the city centre. I strolled into the reception area with its deep-pile carpets and potted plants trying to look confident. As I approached the enquiry desk, the disembodied voice of Dave Delmonte crackled out of a speaker on the wall.

"Hi there. The time is just coming up to ten fifteen. At ten thirty we have the news and weather and, after that, we have a young person from the Radical Christian Fellowship to speak to us about their work. And now for Michael Jackson . . . "

I had this sudden, inexplicable urge to turn straight round and run all the way back home. My legs weakened as I wobbled towards the receptionist. "I'm Julian Christopher," I told her. "For the Dave Delmonte show."

It was a bit like saying, *I'm Julian Christopher and I'm here to be executed.* The receptionist smiled nicely at me then picked up the phone to tell someone I'd arrived. "Would you like a cup of coffee?" she asked. "If you take a seat, there'll be someone down to collect you in a few minutes."

"Thank you. Thank you very much."

I accepted a plastic cup of something warm and wet and milky and carried it over to a coffee table surrounded by low-slung armchairs and piles of glossy magazines. I sat opposite a vicar who was reading the *Financial Times*.

"Good morning," I said politely.

He frowned at me and grunted.

I leafed through some of the magazines; I wanted something to distract me, to stop me feeling nervous, but there was nothing I could concentrate on. I couldn't think of anything less riveting than last month's copy of *Ideal Home* magazine.

The vicar took out his pipe and started filling it with tobacco. Just above his head was a No Smoking sign. I wasn't sure whether to point it out to him or not. I didn't want to seem rude but, on the other hand, I didn't want him to feel guilty when he stood up and saw the notice. He took his matches out and struck one.

I thought I'd better say something. "There's a . . . " I started. But as I moved my hand to point the notice out, I caught the edge of my plastic cup and spilled hot coffee all over the table, the glossy magazines, the vicar's trousers and the pile of papers he'd brought with him.

"Clumsy oaf," he grumbled, tipping the coffee off his papers and on to the Radio Rivelin carpet.

"I am sorry," I said. I took out my hanky to help him wipe his trousers but he seemed more concerned with his pages of notes. "I've worked hours on these," he complained. "I probably won't be able to read a word I've written now."

"I am very sorry," I said again. I felt really stupid. I went to the receptionist and asked her for some tissues for the vicar to clean himself up.

Just then the door opened and a middle-aged bloke wearing skin-tight jeans and a denim shirt walked in. "Hi there!" he said. "Welcome to Radio Rivelin."

The studio was very small. It had a round table with a microphone hanging in the middle and chairs for Dave Delmonte, the vicar and myself. In front of us was a glass partition through which we could see the headphoned technician operating a tape recorder and mixing machine next door.

We listened to the news and weather and then the latest single from Madonna. While the record was playing, Dave asked the vicar and myself what we'd eaten for breakfast. I thought that seemed a bit irrelevant but he explained that it was just to do a sound check so the technician could measure how loud our voices were.

"Well now, that was Madonna, the time is ten thirty-five and here with me in the studio I have the Reverend Oscar Boleham-Wood from St Peter's Church in Chiddleham and Julian Christopher from the Radical Christian Fellowship. Good morning."

The vicar snorted something inaudible at the microphone.

"Good morning," I said, trying to sound confident and cheerful.

"Now Reverend," Dave Delmonte went on, "we've had a complaint from you about the activities of the Radical Christian Fellowship. Perhaps you'd like to tell our listeners what it is exactly you're objecting to."

The vicar took out his pages of notes and peered at the dark brown coffee stains. I was glad that I'd spoiled his script. He couldn't read any of it.

He looked up and frowned at me.

"You received a letter from them . . . " Dave prompted.

"Yes, they've written to us twice," the Reverend grumbled. "Firstly asking us to give furniture, blankets and clothing for this inner city project of theirs and, secondly, asking us for money to send out to people somewhere in Africa."

"And aren't those the kind of projects Christians would be only too glad to help with . . . ?"

"No," said the Reverend.

I looked at him in disbelief.

"What we have to encourage," said the Reverend, "is initiative. These people living in the slums need to get off their backsides and find themselves a job. There's no encouragement to do that when we just give them things on a plate."

I could hardly believe it. I stared at him open mouthed. I felt really angry.

When Dave Delmonte turned to me, I told him about my problems looking for a flat in Rothwell. I told him about the family living huddled together in a room that was smaller than my parents' bathroom.

"And what about the people of Eritrea?" Dave asked the Reverend. "Do you think they ought to get off their backsides and find themselves jobs as well?"

The vicar grunted. "Well, if we keep helping them, they'll never learn to help themselves," he said. "They have to learn to save enough food to keep themselves from droughts."

I was seething. I felt like pulling the plug off the mike and switching the vicar off the air. "That's just not true," I interrupted. "The problem isn't just about drought. They've coped with droughts for thousands of years. Wealthier nations have made the problem worse by lending them money to buy weapons they can't afford. Ethiopia, for instance, pays £4 million a week to the Soviet Union just in interest charges. These people are working flat out to help themselves but nearly all the food they're producing goes in exports – most of it feeding us here in the West."

The vicar tried to interrupt me but I didn't let him. I talked about the meeting we were organizing to raise cash to send to Eritrea. I told people where our new centre was as well. "If you can bring in any furniture you don't want," I told them, "people in Rothwell would be really grateful. Or if you have any bedding – or children's clothes – or toys . . ."

"Well, that's really great," said Dave Delmonte, "but we've got Winny Wittleham waiting with our Tuesday cookery tips, and Petrovelli with the horoscope . . ."

I looked around the studio but there was no one else about. Not unless Winny and Petrovelli were hiding under the table.

"So, I'd like to say a really big thank you to my two special guests: Julian Christopher and the Reverend Oscar Boleham-Wood. Coming up after Cookery Corner we'll be listening to the latest release from Dire Straits, but first of all, over to you Winifred . . ."

As Dave said this, he took off his headphones and we heard the voice of Winny on the speaker telling us how to make gooseberry turnovers.

"Well, thanks a million," said Dave, holding out his hand for us to shake. "It's been great to have both of you on the programme."

"It's a pleasure," I said. "And nice to meet you, Mr Boleham-Wood."

The vicar snorted noisily as I turned towards the door.

After the next meeting of the Christian Fellowship we all went for a drink together in The Crown. There were two main topics of conversation: the picket line and my debut on the radio.

I really enjoyed telling Jamie about my exploits with the Reverend Boleham-Wood. He laughed out loud when I told him about spilling coffee on the vicar's trousers and spoiling his notes. "He must have been livid," Jamie chuckled. "I bet he never volunteers to go on again."

Rog had heard the programme and thought I'd done really well. I hadn't been too sure myself until people started dropping by the centre with furniture, bedding and children's clothes. The others in the group had suggested straightaway that I go round some of the churches, youth clubs and so forth and try to get them to support our different projects. I'd written some letters and fixed up quite a long list of engagements. I was very pleased about it. I felt as if I was doing something useful.

Those of us who'd been on the picket line came in for a lot of criticism. "I thought we'd decided that we'd only get involved in non-violent action," said Adam.

"Well we didn't know how things would turn out," said Meg.

"That's no excuse for Jamie knocking that policeman flying."

Rog frowned. "That's the trouble, isn't it? It's so easy just to get carried away with the crowd. Then you do things you regret straightaway."

Everyone turned to Jamie. There was no expression on his face. He just stared at the wall.

"It was probably an accident," said Cathy. "I'm sure Jamie didn't mean to hurt him."

Everyone waited for Jamie to take up the excuse. His eyes blazed out with anger. "Of course it wasn't a bloody accident," he said. "You didn't see what that copper was doing. He could have smashed Julian's head apart. You can't expect me to just stand there and watch!"

"You could have talked to him," said Adam.

"Talked to him! What the bloody hell would you expect me to say? Say a prayer for him? Read him a passage from the bloody Bible?"

Rog shook his head. "There's no need to talk like that," he said.

Jamie still looked angry. "I'm sorry," he said, "but you can all be so bloody naive sometimes. It's the real fucking world we're living in; not fairyland."

The air was heavy with embarrassment.

"Nobody finds it easy to love their enemies," said Rog, "or to turn the other cheek. But if we call ourselves Christians then that's what we have to aim for."

"Well, I think Jamie might have been right," said Cathy. "And I think we have to trust people to do what they think is best."

Cathy was sitting on the other side of Jamie gazing at him simperingly. She looked up expectantly as if she was waiting for his approval. It had only been four or five weeks ago that she'd been falling about over Andy. I assumed that Andy was out of favour now.

Jamie seemed ill at ease. "I'm going to the bar," he said. "Can I get anyone a drink?"

We all gave our orders in. "Shall I come and help you carry them?" asked Cathy.

"No, you're all right, thanks. I can manage." He stepped out and went to the bar.

When the others carried on talking, Cathy leaned towards me. "Has Jamie got a girlfriend?" she whispered.

I felt increasingly annoyed with her. "I've no idea."

"Well, hasn't he mentioned anybody? You're friendly with him, aren't you?"

I just didn't want to be involved in this conversation. "Why don't you ask him yourself?" I said.

"Well, it's easier to ask you."

"Well, I don't know. He's never talked about it."

"Will you ask him when he comes back?"

I sighed. This was getting stupid. It was like first year kids at school. "You ask him."

"I don't like to."

Jamie started weaving his way towards us with a tray of drinks.

"I'll just go to the toilet," said Cathy confidentially. "You ask him while I'm gone."

She stood up and helped Jamie unload the drinks. As she moved away she looked at me and motioned her head towards Jamie. "Ask him," she mouthed.

Jamie passed the drinks round then sat down next to me. "Are you OK?"

"Mmmmm."

"You look a bit worried."

I liked the way that Jamie noticed things like that. It was one of the things that made it so easy for me to talk to him. "It's Cathy," I said. "She fancies you."

He laughed out loud and patted me on the shoulder. "Poor old Jules," he said. "You lose out every time, don't you?"

I grinned at him and shook my head. "It's all right," I said. "I'm not bothered."

Jamie smiled and shook his head. "I'm sorry about that," he said "That must have made you feel pretty rotten."

"No, no, it's all right. It doesn't matter."

"They can be a real pain sometimes, women."

"I mean, you can go out with her if you want to; it doesn't make any difference to me."

Just then Cathy reappeared.

Jamie got up out of his seat. "I'd better go and have a word with her."

"Honestly, I'm not bothered. I mean, I won't be offended."

"We could fight it out like real men."

"I don't think so, somehow."

"You could challenge me to a duel."

"Go on." I shoved him away.

Jamie took his drink and went over to meet Cathy by the bar.

I couldn't hear the conversation. I just watched it. Jamie took Cathy on one side. He said something to her and Cathy nodded. She looked a bit embarrassed. Jamie smiled and shook his head and started explaining. I hoped he wasn't saying anything about me. I was watching to see whether either of them glanced across at me but they didn't. Then they both laughed. Cathy looked as if she was apologizing. I'd expected the conversation to look difficult and heavy, but it seemed more as if they were sharing a private joke. Jamie put his arm round Cathy and hugged her. It wasn't particularly affectionate; it was more of a gesture of No hard feelings; we're still good friends, aren't we? Then Jamie walked over to the Gents.

When Cathy came and sat down again she was grinning.

I leaned across. "What did he say?"

She smiled and shook her head. "I don't think I ought to tell you."

"Go on."

She hesitated for a moment then she leaned across to me. "Jamie's gay," she whispered.

When I got home I couldn't sleep. I kept thinking about what Cathy had said. I wondered at first if it wasn't true – Jamie might just have said that to put Cathy off. Then I decided that was unlikely. If you announced that you were gay then it would put off women you fancied as well as those you didn't. I couldn't see a straight bloke doing that.

I felt shocked. It wasn't that I had anything against homosexuals; I'd just never thought about them. I'd never needed to before. But suddenly it seemed as if I needed to now. It wasn't just finding out that a friend of mine was gay; it was wondering whether he fancied me or not and, what was more important, whether I fancied him. I didn't know what to think.

The only thing that really worried me was the scene in my flat when we'd come back from the picket. I'd tried not to worry about it because I know that sometimes it's possible to get turned on by all sorts of unlikely things. I remember for instance when I was younger, feeling sexy whenever I travelled on a bus. In fact, I used to find it so embarrassing I used to sit upstairs on my own, even though I disliked the smell of the stale tobacco smoke.

There I'd be, staring down at the empty beer cans and crisp packets strewn across the grimy bus shelter roofs, shuffling constantly in my seat as the vibrations from the double decker juddered through my lower regions. I felt really worried that anyone I knew might get on the bus and sit near me and notice.

At first I thought I must have a fetish about buses. I thought that could be really bad. Then I just stopped worrying. People get turned on by all sorts of different things. It's not as though every time I see a bus I get a hard-on. It doesn't affect me nowadays. So, that's what I told myself about Jamie; just because there was something he'd done that turned me on didn't mean I had to be gay for the rest of my life.

Or did it? I mean, was I? The more I thought about it, the more worried I became. It would explain why I'd felt so embarrassed about my father buying me contraceptives – a normal bloke wouldn't have felt like that. He'd have been really pleased. He'd have probably rushed straight out to find himself a bird to screw. He'd have used all the contraceptives up instead of hiding them round his bedroom. In fact, a normal bloke would have probably finished up asking his father for extra supplies.

I tried hard not to worry. I had lots of other things on my mind because I'd started the month-long schedule of meetings, going round the different churches explaining about our two campaigns to feed the hungry and to help the inner city. I was doing really well. I found it easy to speak to people in public, even though it was something that I'd never had to do before.

I thought about the feeling I'd had when I'd first moved into my flat; the sense of having a mission. I'd seen myself speaking to other people about things that were important and that's what I seemed to be doing. I was pleased about it; it made me feel that I was on the right track. But I didn't feel so sure about Jamie. Was it right that I should carry on seeing him? Was I going to be gay? I didn't know. When I couldn't sort it out, I prayed for God to show me what was right.

I sat down and concentrated all my thoughts and then the quiet voice that came inside my head told me that I should talk to Jamie about it; the longer I ignored the problem, the more difficult it would get. Already, I felt a bit scared of getting close to Jamie and I didn't think that was right. I felt as though some of the others in the group were distancing themselves from him as well. There were things about him that were different. He was more aggressive than the rest of us; his language was violent as well. Nobody was rude to him, but nobody seemed to go out of their way to be friendly towards him either. It was as if people felt that really he didn't belong. I didn't want to feel like that. I liked Jamie. I'd started to value the friendship and it seemed a shame to let it go.

We got so much support for the Food for Eritrea project that we'd decided to call a big public meeting with Paul Richardson, a well-known speaker who'd been working in Africa with Oxfam. We were going to have the meeting in the Free Trade Hall. I'd been asked to say a few words to introduce Paul, and Jamie was organizing the publicity.

"I'd like to have a chat with you about the press releases, Jules," he said on Sunday night.

"OK."

"Shall I come round and show you what I've done so far?"

"Yes. All right."

"Are you free tomorrow night?"

"Mmm," I nodded.

"About half past seven?"

"OK."

I tidied the flat. I wasn't sure why, but I needed to keep myself busy. I knew that when Jamie came, I ought to talk to him about some of the things that were on my mind, but I didn't know what to say. I just hoped that, when the time was right, the words would be right as well.

Jamie turned up with his press releases and a few cans of lager. He'd brought me a tape as well. I'd mentioned to him sometime that I liked Genesis and so he brought me round this tape that had Phil Collins on it.

First of all, we went through the press releases and talked about which papers we ought to send them to. "I was thinking of sending one to the bloke who did the radio programme you were on," said Jamie. "What was his name?"

"Dave Delmonte."

He wrote it down. "We can send one to the local TV station as well. I don't think they'll pick up on it, but it won't do any harm to let them know."

After we'd talked about the publicity, we opened the cans of lager and put on the tape.

I can feel it coming in the air tonight
Oh Lord
And I've been waiting for this moment for all my life . . .

It's one of those records where you always think of the words as being really significant but at the same time you're not sure what they mean. It's a song that seems to have something sexy and erotic about it as well. I started to feel a bit uneasy.

I can feel it coming in the air tonight
Oh Lord

I always find it difficult to talk to people about things that are really personal. What I usually do is think of something that's kind of related to the subject but not quite there. Then I can sort of lead into it gradually.

"Are you getting on all right with Cathy?"

Jamie laughed. "I think so. She's probably after somebody else by now." He grinned at me. "You never know, Jules, it might be your lucky day. It might be your turn next."

I shook my head. "I don't think so."

There was a pause. "Cathy told me what you'd said."

He nodded. He said nothing. I thought Jamie was just going to leave it there. I thought that maybe it would have been better if I hadn't said anything.

I've seen your face before, my friend,
But I don't know if you know who I am.

He took a long drink of his lager. "Does it bother you?"

"No," I said straightaway. Then I realized that that wasn't true. It did bother me but I didn't know how to explain.

"You look a bit uncertain."

There was a longer pause then. "Have you always been gay?" I asked him.

Jamie paused. "Mm . . . I suppose so. I've often wondered. I mean, I don't know that people are born gay. Maybe some are but with me I think it was mainly that I went to an all-boys school and it just went on there all the time. None of us thought about being gay – it was just what everybody did at school."

I nodded.

"I got into a more serious relationship. I fell in love." He stared at the carpet for a moment. "We were best friends and then it just developed. I did worry about that because . . . because I knew I was taking it so seriously. When I came home from school in the holidays, I tried going out with girls but I just didn't feel at ease with women. It might have been because I'd never had girls as friends. I always thought of them as being like a different species. If I went out with a girl I had to be thinking of the right things to say and how to make conversation with her. With Rob, my friend – my lover – it was different. We just got on great. There was this real kind of bond between us. We could almost read each other's thoughts."

"Hey, that's really funny, I had a friend as well. He was called Rob. He was like that – I mean – it was that same sort of relationship. As if I could tell what he was thinking – read what was going through his mind. It's a coincidence." I thought about it. "I suppose it's a common enough name, though. There must be lots of people called Rob."

Jamie nodded. As he looked up, there was a tiny . . . I don't know . . . it was just that, for a minute fraction of a second, he looked guilty. "What happened to your friend?" he asked me.

I hesitated. "He died."

Jamie looked sympathetic. "You must have missed him."

"Yes."

I paused. I wondered if I could have been in love as well. I'd never thought of my friendship with Rob as being gay. I just thought we were friends. I didn't feel so sure about it now. I felt confused. "What happened to your . . ." I found the word hard to say, "your lover?"

Jamie smiled. "He's married now. He's got a couple of kids. We go out for a drink together sometimes."

I poured myself another glass of lager. "Didn't you go out with women later on?" I asked Jamie. "When you left school?"

"Well, I went to Sandhurst and there aren't too many women there."

"Sandhurst? Isn't that something to do with the army?"

"That's right. It's an officer training school." He gave me a sheepish grin. "I hadn't told you I was in the army."

I must have looked incredulous. "No."

"It doesn't quite fit in with the Radical Christian bit, does it?"

"Well, everybody can change their mind about things."

Jamie nodded. "That's right."

I can feel it coming in the air tonight
Oh Lord
And I've been waiting for this moment for all my life . . .

We sat and listened to Phil Collins and it felt good to be talking to Jamie and sorting things out; there were still other things I felt as though I ought to talk about but I didn't know how to say them.

When the tape finished, Jamie drained his glass of lager. He turned to me. "Look, Jules," he said, "I feel as though I want to clear the air a bit. I mean, I want to be frank with you."

I nodded.

"I don't want to offend you or . . . I don't want to say anything that might get in the way of . . . well, of our being friends. Friendships are important to me. It's good to meet people I can get on with. It's really great just to have somebody around to talk to."

I nodded.

"I don't want the fact that I'm gay to come between us. I

don't want it to spoil things." He moved towards me and rested his hand on my shoulder. "I do like you, Jules, and I do find you attractive. I can't get away from that. The fact that I'm gay means that I'm bound to see that extra dimension in any relationship I have with a bloke. I can't help that."

I nodded. I didn't know what to say.

"Does that disturb you?"

"No. No, I'm pleased you feel that you can talk about it."

He nodded. "Good." He emptied the rest of the lager into his glass. "I don't know enough about you, Jules. I mean, you've told me something about your relationships with women but, obviously . . . there are other things I don't know anything about like this relationship with Rob. I don't know what that was like for you . . . "

He paused and took a drink.

"If you do feel, if you ever should feel that . . . well, that your friendship with me could ever reach into . . . well, if you think you might like to try out . . . something different. I mean, I'll just leave that up to you. I wouldn't want to hassle you in any way."

I shook my head. "I don't feel hassled."

"That's OK." He squeezed my shoulder gently. "But the important thing is that, whatever you feel about things, we can still be friends."

It was a question. "Yes, that's important to me."

When I went to bed that night I felt OK. I felt as though it had been good to talk to Jamie and I was pleased to have got things sorted out. By next morning I was paranoid.

I had dreamed that Jamie was making love to me. I was a little boy in hospital and Jamie was the doctor. He entered my cubicle wearing a white overall with a large thermometer bulging out of his pocket. When I lay down on my bed, Jamie came and folded back the sheets. Then he bent over me and started unbuttoning my pyjamas. I felt relaxed and I trusted him. It was beautifully erotic. Then Jamie started petting me and stroking me. I woke up throbbing, my senses dizzy with the warm stickiness of sleeping sex until the wash of fear plunged me backwards.

That was it, I said to myself when I woke up. I'd found myself out at last. I'd discovered myself in the closet. I was gay.

My soul sank. I wanted to go back to the person I was before I had the dream, but that person wasn't there. The Julian who hadn't had the dream was lost and gone for ever. I had to find the person who'd come along to take his place.

I lay in bed, struggling to be gay. Trying to put on the persona, slip myself inside the skin. What did gay blokes think about? How did they behave? What did they do when they got out of bed?

I couldn't imagine. I didn't really know.

I thought of the caricatures on TV, the blokes in drag. I thought of myself with a handbag, mincing down the street. Could I still be Julian Christopher and be gay? I didn't know. I didn't know what would become of me.

I forced myself out of bed and staggered over to the mirror. I felt as though I must have undergone a transformation. There must be something different I could notice, like discovering soft down, quietly growing like emerging pubic hair on the palms of my hands.

It still looked like me in the mirror, the me I'd always known. Or had I? Had I ever known myself? I didn't feel as if I knew myself now. I wasn't sure who I was.

I dressed myself in my jeans and sweat shirt. Perhaps there had always been something about me, about the way I dressed, the way I walked, or the way I spoke. Something that pointed me out. Something I wasn't aware of. Something that was different.

When I walked down the street to the shops, I tried looking at other blokes. It wasn't so easy to fancy them. I tried to imagine them without their clothes, the way I sometimes found myself doing with girls. But I didn't know which parts of men you were supposed to find attractive.

It was really embarrassing when one bloke turned round and smiled at me. I think he must have guessed what I was thinking. I didn't know where to put myself. I was in the queue at the chemist's at the time and I'd intended asking for some talcum powder and a packet of soft toilet rolls. I finished up buying one roll of Izal medicated and came out without the talc. I decided that, even if I was gay, I'd have to stay in the closet a little while longer.

Another problem I had was that I wasn't absolutely sure what gay blokes did. I mean, what they did together. In bed. Or wherever else they did it. I mean, I had a few ideas but I wasn't really certain. I knew what you were supposed to do with women and even then I'd never got it right. What hope did I have of getting it right with a bloke?

But, maybe I didn't find men attractive after all.

Maybe I wasn't a homosexual.

Maybe my problem was that I was just falling in love with Jamie.

Jamie came round to see me again to sort out the details for the public meeting. "I've had a phone call from Radio Rivelin," he announced. "Dave Delmonte wants Paul Richardson on his chat show on Friday morning. He'd like you to be there as well. Is that OK?"

"Yes, that's fine." I said. "I had thought about going to Astonbury, but I'm not bothered. I mean, it doesn't matter."

The Christian Peace Movement had organized a Good Friday service to be held outside the US base at Astonbury. Most of the people from the Fellowship were travelling over there in a minibus on the Friday morning. I had thought I'd like to go but it wasn't that important.

I showed Jamie the speech I'd written. It was only short because people would be coming to hear Paul Richardson, not me. "That looks fine," said Jamie. "You don't want to go on for too long, do you? This looks just about right."

"I hope so."

I put my papers back inside my folder. "Would you like some coffee?"

"Thanks. That'd be great."

I put the kettle on.

We chatted some more about arrangements for the meeting, then we sat down with our coffee on the floor.

It was Jamie who brought things back to what we'd been talking about before. He wasn't as shy as I was. "I was thinking," he said, "about the other night. I wondered if I'd said the wrong thing. I thought . . . I don't know . . . I wondered if you might have been offended."

"No. No, of course not."

"Are you sure?"

When he looked at me straight in the eye, I felt strangely shy and embarrassed. I smiled and nodded at him briefly, then I stared down at my coffee.

"What I think I do find a bit difficult . . ." I started.

"Mmmmm . . . ?"

"Is that, well, I feel as if I haven't got myself sorted out – like, as far as sex is concerned. I mean, I'm not quite sure what my own sort of . . ." I didn't know how to put it. "Like, which way I'm . . ." I didn't know how to explain.

"Go on."

I stared down at my coffee mug. The thoughts were all there in my head but I couldn't fit words around them.

"You can trust me, you know." There was silence. "Look, Jules, like I said, friendship's very important to me.

That means having someone you can confide in."

I nodded.

"You're not afraid of me, are you?"

That was half the trouble: there was something about Jamie that was . . . I didn't know. I did feel afraid of him. I just nodded.

He shifted nearer to me and rested his hand on my shoulder. "Come on, Jules. If there's things you want to tell me, then just say them. You can trust me, can't you?"

I wanted to trust in Jamie but my mind blanked out. I wanted to float away. The thoughts were there, large as life, inside my head, but I couldn't find words to go with them. I almost felt like crying. I wouldn't allow myself to cry with Jamie because I didn't want him to see me so defenceless. I stared down at my coffee and said nothing.

Jamie seemed to understand. He put his arm round my shoulders and hugged me. I wasn't sure how to respond to that. I just reached up and squeezed his wrist.

There was a longer silence then. Jamie kept his arm around my shoulder but took a long drink of his coffee.

"Julian," he said slowly, "do you think that might be why you've never got on too well with women – is that what you're saying?"

I said nothing.

"I don't want to push you into anything, but if you feel as though there are things you want to sort out . . . do you know what I mean?"

I nodded.

"If you think it might be helpful . . . I don't want to put any pressure on you. I mean, you're younger than I am . . . you're not as experienced . . . I wouldn't want to take advantage in any way."

I nodded again. I felt stupid, not saying anything, but I knew that, in a way, that was what I wanted. I did want to trust in Jamie. I wanted him to take control.

He squeezed my shoulder. "Come on, it'll be all right."

I looked up and smiled at him weakly.

"It might be good for you just to kind of try things out and then see how you feel. I mean, the last thing I would want is to push you. I mean, I wouldn't want to put you under any sort of pressure."

I nodded.

"You just want to find out who you are. Don't you?"

Just then the phone rang in the downstairs hall. I let it ring. A short time later I heard footsteps climbing to the attic. There was a knock on the door. "Phone call for you, Julian."

It was Winston, the black guy from the ground floor flat. "Thanks, Winston," I said. "Sorry to put you out."

I went down to take the phone call. It was Dave Delmonte. "I'd like to check the time for Friday's interview," he said. "Would you mind coming on towards the last part of the show – about half past twelve?"

"That'll be OK."

I talked about Paul Richardson and the arrangements for the meeting, but my mind was with Jamie in the attic. What was I supposed to do? What was going to happen next? Had I agreed to go to bed with him? I wasn't sure. And was he expecting to do that now, like when I got upstairs? And what were we supposed to do together? I didn't know that either.

"I'll look forward to seeing you on Friday."

"OK."

I wanted to keep the conversation going. I was scared of going back upstairs. I wanted to talk to somebody about it. I bet Dave Delmonte knew what gay blokes did in bed together.

"Cheers, then."

"Bye."

I replaced the receiver and turned to walk upstairs.

When I walked back into the attic, Jamie was standing by the door with his coat on and his car keys in his hand. I breathed out a sigh of relief. I'd half expected to find him lying naked on my bed.

"I'll be off now," he said.

"OK."

"Are you doing anything Friday evening?"

I shook my head.

"Do you fancy having a meal?"

"That'd be nice."

"I do a nice line in vegetable curry. Do you fancy a curry?"

"Yes, that'd be great."

He put his hand on my shoulder, the way he did before. "We'll have a meal together on Friday." He paused. "Look, you don't have to do anything you don't want to do." He looked straight into my eyes. "You know that, don't you?"

I nodded, but I wasn't absolutely sure.

"I'll see myself out. Thanks for the coffee. And I'll see you at the meeting on Thursday."

"OK. Bye."

"Bye."

I let Jamie walk to the front door by himself.

I did all the things I normally did: I ate breakfast and I brushed my hair; I hoovered the floor of my room and put disinfectant down the sink. I did all the things I always did, but the person doing them had changed. I was growing a new identity.

I was trying to plan out Thursday's meeting. I'd been arranging it for the last few weeks: sending out invitations to different groups, designing posters and leaflets, advertising in the press. Now my mind couldn't concentrate on Thursday any longer. All I could think about was Jamie: Jamie and me on Friday.

I felt excited and light-headed. I remembered when I was very small and we were going on holiday in an aeroplane. I'd never flown in one before. Each time I thought about it, my tummy started turning over. I felt a bit scared, because I knew aeroplanes could crash and so my excitement was a mixture of happiness and fear. I remembered, on the day before the holiday, running out of school with my arms spreading wide, wheeling and diving. I was playing at being an aeroplane.

I don't know what it is that makes us want to play at being the things we're most afraid of. I don't know if I needed to play at being gay in the same way that I needed to play at being an aeroplane. I don't know whether I was playing or if I was falling in love.

I found myself thinking about Rob. When Jamie told me that he'd had a lover called Rob, it reminded me of the comradeship that I never really appreciated until after it was gone.

Rob seemed like the only other person that I'd ever felt really close to. My parents had always said they loved me and I knew that they cared about me, but they'd always been much too busy to find out who I was. Clare hadn't loved me; I was just a boy at school she fancied; Kerry Ann was a girl I fancied. I wasn't in love with her. And I felt pleased I'd never got really attached to Cathy. She was just sleeping round all the blokes she knew; I didn't want to be included on her list.

With Jamie, for the first time, I had the possibility of something deeper. I felt a bit scared because Jamie was older than me and more experienced. In some ways he made me feel very unsure of myself. I tried to believe that whatever I did with him would be OK. All I had to do was trust in him and be myself.

Thursday's meeting was massive. The Free Trade Hall was packed out with people. I could hardly believe it when I saw them. They were buying books and pamphlets, examining our exhibition boards which described the project we were supporting in Eritrea and queuing up to covenant money. At half past seven everyone moved into the rows of seats and I walked on to the platform to introduce Paul Richardson.

I gazed out at the rows of faces and felt a buzzing of success. I felt privileged to be in the presence of so many people who cared about what was happening. I began by thanking everyone: all the churches and other groups who'd pledged us their support and everyone who'd helped to make the meeting a success. On the front row were some journalists, taking shorthand notes and two press photographers kept walking forward, adjusting exposure meters and taking photographs. I was on the stage some time before I noticed Jamie, standing at the back. When my eyes met his he smiled at me. I felt a bit shaky; I don't know why. I smiled back at him. I carried on speaking about the other work of the Radical Christian Fellowship, mentioning about the minibuses to Astonbury the following day; but all the time I felt conscious of Jamie being there, in the audience. I found myself avoiding him, looking up and down the rows of faces but turning back before my eyes caught his.

I finished off by introducing Paul Richardson. I had a little card on which I'd written the names of his various books and the places where he'd worked. I read it all out and then said, "Over to you, Paul," and sat down. Everyone applauded.

I felt more at ease when Paul was speaking. I looked around the audience and thought what a good job we'd done. I felt really pleased that so many people had turned out. When I'd called in home a couple of weeks before I'd told my mum and dad about the meeting. They said they'd try to get along but I felt sure they'd be too busy. Anyway, I didn't mind them not being there. Like Jamie had said, I wanted a different set of people to feel proud of me now.

When Paul finished, we had fifteen minutes or so of questions. After that I thanked Paul and then thanked everyone once again for coming. I told them we were serving tea and biscuits afterwards. Everyone clapped again.

I felt pleased when I walked down off the stage. I'd put a lot of work into the meeting and everything had turned out well. I was feeling quite elated.

Jamie had walked down to the front. He was waiting at the side of the stage with the journalists and photographers. They were mostly wanting to interview Paul Richardson but some of them were waiting to speak to me. Before they could get near, Jamie walked up to me and put his arms around me. I didn't mind too much about that. I was feeling happy and excited and it seemed natural and nice to have a friend to share it with. Jamie hugged me and then he held me back a little way and he looked at me. I didn't try to move away from him or anything, I just felt slightly puzzled. Then he kissed me. He kissed me on my mouth. It wasn't a long kiss but it was in public in front of all the people. I suppose I must have closed my eyes. I felt shell-shocked. I didn't know what to do. I looked at Jamie and he smiled at me. It was strange to see his face so closely. I noticed the wrinkles round the corners of his eyes and a scar on his upper lip, almost hidden by his moustache. I'd never noticed that before because I'd never stood so close to him. Jamie didn't say anything at all; he held my arms for a moment, almost pinning them down by my sides, then he turned and walked away.

There was silence for a few seconds. I suppose the journalists were quite shocked. They looked at Jamie and then they looked at me and, when I just stared vacantly back at them, they started their interviews, asking me about the Food for Eritrea project and the action we'd planned at Astonbury. I answered the questions like an android. I didn't feel elated any more; all I was aware of was the smell and taste of Jamie on my mouth. I wanted to wipe it away. I put my hand in my pocket, pulled out a handkerchief and wiped it round my mouth. I looked down at the handkerchief. It was splattered with blood. It was Jamie's handkerchief, the one he'd used to wipe up the blood from my cuts the day we were outside on the picket.

I wanted to go home. I felt suddenly confused as if I wasn't sure what was happening. Something seemed to be wrong. I wanted to sit down on my own and quietly sort things out. Everyone was busy, drinking tea and chatting. The journalists went over to interview Paul Richardson. No one seemed to be noticing me. There was a side door next to me marked EXIT. I checked again that no one was watching then I walked quickly through the door and went home.

The next day was Good Friday and I had to meet Paul Richardson and take him to Radio Rivelin.

We walked into the foyer and I found Paul a seat while I went to tell the receptionist we'd arrived. Then I collected a cup of coffee for him. "You seem to know your way around," he said.

I nodded. I could have told him about the interview I'd had the other week. I could have told him how nervous I was and about how I spilled my coffee over the vicar's trousers. I just didn't feel like talking.

The interview went smoothly. Dave Delmonte asked me a few questions and then talked to Paul about his work with Oxfam and about the drought in Africa. I stared around the studio. I looked through the glass panel in the wall to where the technician was sorting out his records. I looked at the rows of neatly-catalogued spools of tape and the in-trays filled with record requests from Dave Delmonte's fans.

"Don't you agree, Julian?"

I glanced up at Dave who was waiting for me to answer his question. I'd no idea what he'd asked me.

"Er . . . yes, I think so," I stammered.

Dave Delmonte smiled and nodded. "Well, thank you very much for bringing Paul Richardson here to meet us all," I looked around the studio. There was still only Dave and the technician.

"It's been a pleasure."

"Well, I hope we'll see you again before too long, Julian, and the best of luck with all your work."

"Thank you."

"And we'll finish off the programme with Dire Straits singing 'Brothers in Arms'."

I took Paul Richardson to the station and saw him to his train. I didn't feel like going straight home so I went for a walk in the park.

The park was near where Jamie lived. I'd never been there before. In fact, I never knew where Jamie lived before but now I had his address in my Filofax. I took out the piece of card on which he'd written it down. In five hours' time I was due there.

The park had flower beds and trees and a row of children's swings. There was nobody on the swings. It had a hill in the middle with a monument on the top and behind the trees was a building that looked like a small museum. I climbed up the hill to the monument. It was very disappointing. It was a war memorial with a list of the names of men who'd died in the two world wars and a notice which just said, Olive Mount. I stood for a few moments by the side of the plaque but in whichever direction I looked there was nothing to see. Everything was cloudy. It seemed as if it was just about to rain. I set off down the hill towards the trees.

As I walked down the hillside, I looked about me and wondered which was Jamie's flat. I felt suddenly ill at ease. I thought of Jamie, watching me, looking out of his window, the way I sometimes stared down at passers-by from my attic. I found the thought disturbing. It was like an invasion of my privacy. I felt as if Jamie's eyes were on me and I wanted to wipe them away in the same way that I'd wanted to wipe away the taste of him with the handkerchief.

I heard the low distant rumbling of thunder and I hurried on towards the building behind the trees.

I couldn't understand why Jamie had suddenly become a threat. I tried to make myself see sense. Jamie was my friend. He wanted to be my lover. I was going round to his flat that evening to share a meal with him and afterwards the two of us would probably sleep together in his bed.

The air was getting heavy. I found myself sweating and took my jacket off to walk up the pathway to the building. I felt strangely claustrophobic. There was a tension in the air around me. There was another roll of thunder and then the first few drops of rain spattered in front of me on the path. The storm was about to start.

The small white building was a library, not a museum. It was warm and cosy. I stood inside and watched the rain splash down the windows in a streaming avalanche. I felt safe. I remembered how I used to run home from school when I was little whenever I heard the thunder. I used to love to watch the lightning but only when I felt really safe and secure, with the doors shut and the windows fastened, locked inside my house.

When the librarian walked in, I felt obliged to look through the shelves of books. It didn't seem right to shelter in a library and just stare out through the window.

I wondered if they might have books on homosexuality. I thought that possibly someone might have written a book about the same kind of problems that I had. I scoured the shelves for something called, *How to Tell if You Are*

Homosexual or Not, but of course I couldn't see one. Then I tried the catalogue. I was surprised to find that homosexuality came under the heading of sexual perversions. I hadn't thought of myself as a pervert. They were the sort of people who abused little children and made indecent phone calls or went flashing in the park. I found it all a bit disturbing.

I spent the next ten minutes reading about sexually transmitted diseases and how easy it is to contract AIDS. I read about all the precautions you have to take. It explained that it's best if you have sex without making any contact with people's bodily secretions. I thought that sounded difficult.

Everything seemed sordid. I thought that falling in love would be ennobling, something that lifted me out of myself and made me a better person. I didn't want to make love if I thought it might make me feel disgusted. I didn't know what to do.

Part of me really wanted to try things out, but the rest of me was becoming more and more uncertain. I couldn't stop thinking about the way that Jamie kissed me. I didn't know if I might have enjoyed it if we'd been on our own in private, but I didn't feel ready for being marked out like that in public.

I looked at my watch; it was three o'clock. I was planning on going back to my flat, getting washed and changed then picking up a bottle of wine to take with me to Jamie's. What if I called round there now? I could pop in and have a chat; I could tell him what was on my mind. If we sat down and talked about things over a cup of coffee then I'd feel more relaxed about coming back in the evening.

I took out the scrap of card on which Jamie'd written his address: Flat 15, St Hilda's Walk, Olive Mount Avenue. There were several blocks of flats that overlooked the park. I gazed through the window and wondered which was his.

I didn't know what to do. It was still raining heavily outside so I sat at one of the tables and started writing up my diary. When I have a spare fifteen minutes sometimes, I write out pages in my Filofax and then take them out and put them in my proper diary when I get home.

I looked up when the sun started shining again. The rain had stopped and the library was getting busy. I put my books back on the shelves and waited until the librarian was free. Then I went across and showed her the card with the address. She led me over to the window and pointed out a building opposite the park. I thanked her and walked back to my table.

I looked outside. The sun was streaming through the window. The park was glistening. I could almost smell the heavy scent of rain-soaked grass. I finished off my diary. I looked towards Jamie's flat and put the card back in my Filofax.

I smiled to myself. There was no need to worry any more. I get over anxious sometimes. Everything was going to be all right.

I'm starting to let the mask slip. Normally, I'm cool and cautious, hiding inside a role. Not just one role, lots of roles. Living inside a play. What I sometimes forget is that hiding inside the roles is me. It's easy to get so out of touch with myself that I can't remember what I'm like. But then bits of me leak out. Sometimes I over-spill. The barriers start to break down and I begin to remember who I am.

I start feeling happy and excited. I find it hard to concentrate. I've been working on the file, typing up my report, but then my mind keeps whirling back to Julian. I want to get everything ready. I want to prepare the meal and tidy the flat, have a shower and buy some wine. I want to check out the tapes. I leave the file open on the table and start to prepare the curry. I concentrate on pressing the garlic and chopping up the mushrooms then I go through the list of spices and check that I've got everything to hand. Then I put a record on. I take the Phil Collins out of the sleeve, the record I taped for Julian, and I place it on the deck. Then I start feeling hungry.

Normally everything I do is well thought out. I like to have a routine, doing things in order. Today I'm feeling scatterbrained, flitting from one thing to another. I leave the record on the turntable but forget to put the arm down because then I decide to make myself a plate of chips. I open a can of lager and then I put the chip pan on. I peel a potato and set it on one side then I start on the mushrooms again. It's thundering outside.

I look out of the window and it's starting to pour with rain. I realize that my shirt is clinging to me. The weather's been close and humid and I feel reeky and sticky with sweat. I decide to take a shower.

I was intending to have my shower later, just before Julian arrived but it might be better if he isn't knocked back by the smell of shampoo and after-shave as soon as he walks in. I want to seem casual. I don't want to put him off.

I take off my clothes and I get in the shower and I scrub myself all over. Everything's going to be great. I feel pleased with myself, the way I've handled the situation. I think I've done everything just right. I knew from the start what Julian was like and I knew what his weaknesses were. I've found myself exploiting that but I'm not doing anything to hurt him. I'll be very gentle with him. I want him to fall in love with me.

I spend a long time washing myself. It's easy to forget about scrubbing your back and washing behind your ears. I'm always very particular. I like to be really clean. I shampoo my hair and rinse it and put some conditioner on then I have one final rinse and switch the shower off and start to dry myself.

Suddenly I remember that the off-licence closes early. I remember that they had a notice up saying how they were closing early on Good Friday because they were going away for Easter. I have to buy some wine. We need something to drink with the meal. We don't want just to have lager. I put my clothes on quickly then walk into the living room to get my wallet out of my jacket pocket.

The whole room is dense with thick black smoke. I can hardly see a thing. At first I can't understand what's happened, then I realize: I've left the chip pan on. I take the pan off the cooker then open the door and windows wide. The smoke is so thick I start choking. I put my head out of the window to get my breath. The black smoke billows out. They can probably see it down there in the park. I hope no one phones for the fire brigade. I take a few deep breaths and then I remember about the off-licence. I could nip down there while the smoke clears up. I pick my keys out of my pocket and walk out the door. I decide to leave it open. I won't be gone more than three or four minutes. If I let some air in, the smoke might have cleared when I come back.

I press the button for the lift but it seems to be in use. I can't be bothered waiting. I can run down the stairs in no time. I haven't got my watch on and I'm panicking that the off-licence might be closed already. I sprint down all the stairs.

There are two people in front of me at the off-licence buying in crates of beer for a party. I start to get impatient. I find myself tugging on my earlobe and then stop myself. I tap my foot instead.

I buy the wine and then I dash back to the flats. I press the buttons for both lifts and wait to see which comes down first. I hum a tune to myself as I watch the numbers glow. Someone else has pressed the button on floor five. The left hand lift goes 7 . . . 6 . . . 5 . . . then stops. The right hand lift goes 4 . . . 3 . . . 2 . . . 1 . . . G. I walk inside and press floor five.

Going up in the lift I start to relax. I've got the wine now. Everything's going to be OK. I leave the lift and walk down the terrace to my flat. The door is only partly open. I stop still. I remember leaving it wide open to get rid of all the smoke. It was a stupid, idiotic thing to do but I did it. I hesitate. The air is very still; there isn't any wind, not even a breeze, not enough to move a heavy door. I pause at the doorway and look cautiously inside.

The smoke has cleared now and the first thing I notice is the file and my report, left out on the table. I curse myself. I've never done that before; I've never done anything like that before. I'm always so careful, ultra cautious. Everything is normally locked away and here I am today, walking out of the flat, leaving the door wide open and everything out on the table.

I try to think things out as rationally as I can. How long have I been gone? Four minutes? Five minutes? Six? Certainly no more. Has anybody seen me going out? Has somebody been watching me, waiting for me to leave? It seems unlikely. And who do I know that could have been here? I give my address to nobody. Except Julian, of course. I gave my address to him.

I take a long deep breath and hold on to the doorframe to steady myself. I'll have to go inside and get a drink. I peer cautiously round the door. There could be someone here.

It's very quiet. I think it's empty. I open the door as quietly as I can; I look carefully round the room and then I walk inside. The smoke has just about cleared now but there's still a smell of burning oil.

I'm about to put the wine bottle down, then I change my mind. I take it with me towards the bathroom. I hold the bottle behind me by its neck as I shove the bathroom door open with my foot. There's no one there. I check inside the shower, then I come out and check the living room again. I look behind the curtains and under the settee. I even look in my wardrobe. I'm on my own. I put the wine bottle down on the table and then I open a can of lager.

I sit down and try to think things out. I've been out what . . . ? Five, six minutes? Would that have given Julian time to come up in the lift, time to find a strange flat in a place he'd never been before? Possibly. And if he saw the door was open he'd have probably come inside. He'd have knocked. Then, when there was no answer, he'd have come inside. The file would be right there on the table, straight in front of him. He must have seen it. I feel the dread mounting in my stomach. I have another drink of lager.

I have to think things out. I mustn't panic. I always stay calm. I take a deep breath. The chances of Julian coming here are very very small. There could be some other explanation for the door. Maybe one of the neighbours smelled the smoke and came over to see if I was on fire. I should have thought of that when I went out. I can't believe I could do anything so stupid as to go out leaving the door to my flat wide open. It's just not like me at all.

I think about phoning Julian. Just a nice friendly chat. What time is he coming over? I'm looking forward to seeing him. Perhaps I could ask him to bring me a tape over or a record. Some excuse like that. As soon as I heard his voice on the phone I could tell if there was something wrong.

I go through the conversation in my mind. "Hi, Jules. Are

you OK?" And then I'd wait for the hesitation. I could ask what he'd been doing. Tell him I'd listened to the interview on the radio, ask him what time Paul Richardson left. I could work out whether he'd have had time to come round here or not. If he seemed at all uneasy I could say that I was coming out to Rothwell and offer to pick him up. If I could only talk to him face to face, I'd be able to reassure him. If he has been here and seen the file, I'd have to break down and confess. I think I could bring that off. I'd spin him some yarn about how much I hated the job, the terrible pressure I was under. Confide in him about state conspiracy. I think he'd be sympathetic. He'd be shocked at first but then, if I played my cards right, I think I could make him feel sorry for me.

I phone Julian's number but I get no answer. I let the phone ring and ring because I know it takes him a long time to come down the stairs from the attic. I replace the receiver and then I try again. It could have been a wrong number. There's no answer still. I have another drink of lager.

I wonder if I could have been mistaken about the door. Could I have left it wide open at first and then changed my mind and closed it slightly? Would anyone else have come round? I don't normally give anybody my address. The postwoman? Do they have a post on Good Friday? I'm not sure. The milkman? But neither of them would come without leaving me some letters or a yogurt and a couple of pints of milk.

I don't know who, if anybody, moved the door. I can't assume that it was Julian and I've got to carry on as if nothing had happened. I've got to set the table and finish cooking the meal and put the wine out. I walk over to the hi-fi. The turntable is going round with the record on it still. I lower the pick-up arm.

I start to chop up the vegetables for the curry and I put them to simmer in a pan. I don't bother making any chips. I don't feel hungry any more.

I can feel it coming in the air tonight
Oh Lord

I put a little cooking oil in the frying pan, I roll it round and start to fry the mushrooms.

And I've been waiting for this moment for all my life . . .

I leave the vegetables to simmer and then walk into the bathroom. I pick up my wet towel from the floor and then wipe around the shower. I replace the top on the shampoo and on the conditioner. I put the soap back in its dish. I walk back into the kitchen.

Well, if you told me you were drowning
I would not lend a hand.
I've seen your face before, my friend,
But I don't know if you know who I am.

By eight o'clock I start to think that Julian might not be coming. By half past eight I'm starting to feel certain. The hollow dread is growing in my stomach. I know there's something wrong. I think about eating a plate of curry, but I'm still not feeling hungry. I'll leave it till nine o'clock.

I phone Julian's number again. Winston answers the phone. "I'm sorry to bother you," I tell him. "Would you mind checking whether Julian's in?"

"I'll go up and see," says Winston. I can tell by the tone of his voice that he's been walking up and down stairs calling different tenants to the phone for most of the day. If I lived on the ground floor I think I'd just leave the phone off the hook.

I hear his footsteps fading on the stairs. I hear him calling Julian then, when there's no answer, the footsteps start again but fainter. He's walking up to Julian's room. I strain my ears to hear him knock on Julian's door, but it's all too far away. There is only one set of heavy footsteps coming back.

"No, I'm sorry. He seems to be out."

"Oh." I'm wondering whether to leave a message.

"Actually, I think he went out earlier on. I've not heard him come back."

"What time was that?"

"About five o'clock."

Five o'clock! That's nearly four hours ago. "OK." I tell him. "Thanks a lot."

"Cheers, mate."

"Bye."

I told myself I was going to eat some curry. I can't think well on an empty stomach. The curry is getting dried up now and sticking to the bottom of the pan. I serve myself a helping and sit down with my plate in front of the TV. I'll watch the nine o'clock news. I'll relax while I eat my plate of curry and then, when I've watched the news, I'll get my brain working and sort out what to do.

The main news item is about the postal strike. We see bulging sacks of unopened mail and listen to the complaints of people who are waiting for airline tickets, visas, social security payments and repeat prescriptions. I think it's a national disgrace. They ought to get the army in. I don't think people ought to be allowed to go on strike.

I munch away at my curry. It doesn't taste too bad. Julian doesn't know what he's missing.

> Several people have been arrested after an incident this evening outside the US air base at Astonbury. Members of the Christian Campaign for Nuclear Disarmament and the Radical Christian Fellowship, who held a Good Friday service outside the base this afternoon, blockaded the entrance as cruise missile launchers were brought out on what was described by officials as a routine exercise.

I look up at the TV screen. The picture shows a mass of people sitting down outside the gates. There are banners and placards. I can't see anyone I know.

> One of the peace protesters was injured after being knocked down by a police motor cyclist. The young man, who has not been named, was sitting in the path of the motor bike which was leading the cruise convoy. The young man has been taken to hospital in Oxford.

Julian.

I don't know why I should think it's him, but I do. It's a stupid idea. He wasn't supposed to be going to Astonbury; he was supposed to be coming here. But still I feel the heavy weight of impending doom falling through my stomach. I tell myself I'm being stupid but my thoughts are blocked by the roar of a motor-bike engine as it revs inside my skull. I take hold of a cushion and I place it behind my head because I can already feel the stinging grit from the roadway as it scrapes along my cheek. I've got to pull myself together.

I take my plate over to the sink and start to do some washing up. I turn on the hot tap and I rinse out the pans with cold water. When the water runs warmer, I fill up the bowl and squirt in some Fairy Liquid. I think about the guy I used to know who kept teasing me about using Fairy Liquid. He thought it was a big joke. I've never found it all that funny. I like to keep the skin smooth on my hands.

I always wash the drinking glasses first and then they don't finish up with any greasy marks. I like things to be clean. I like to do a job properly. Did they say the bloke was seriously injured? I can't remember. They said he was in hospital. They said he's not been named. They do that when someone's died and they haven't told their family yet. I don't want Julian to die.

I rinse the glasses under the tap before I stand them on the rack. I never use a tea towel. I think they spread germs.

I try to think what might have gone through Julian's mind if he did come round here and see the file. The first thing he would really notice would be the copy of his diary on the table. He would have been upset. He wouldn't know what to do. He wouldn't know who to talk to. He wouldn't have come to see me this evening because he wouldn't know what to say. He could still have gone to Astonbury. The minibus would have gone but he could still have taken a coach or gone part way on the train. He could even afford to take a taxi. What time did Winston say he went out? Five o'clock? It only takes an hour or so to get there. He would be upset; he might be feeling a bit hysterical. Maybe he'd have a bit to drink . . .

I try to pull myself together. There's no reason for me to think it might be him that's injured. I have to stop being paranoid, just because Julian hasn't turned up. I look at the clock. It's nine twenty-five, maybe he's just late. But if he was going to be late, I tell myself, he'd have phoned me up, let me know he'd been delayed. I pick up the phone to check I haven't left the receiver off. It buzzes. There's nothing wrong with the phone. Julian won't be coming now.

I have to take control of the situation. I have to decide what to do. I don't ever panic. I always stay calm. My main qualification for doing this job is that I always stay cool in a crisis. I'm in a crisis now and I have to make sure I stay calm.

So what do I do next? Should I phone up the hospital and find out the name of the injured bloke? That would be stupid. I've got no reason to do that. Should I call round to see Julian's parents and see what they know? But what if he's told them? What if he's been here and seen the file and he's been round and talked to his mother and father about it, asking them what to do?

I can't keep phoning his flat. Winston won't be too happy to climb the stairs again. What I need to do is go round to his flat and find any evidence I can, anything at all. Maybe there'll be a telephone message. Maybe his mum's been taken ill. There could be a telegram or a phone message, there could be a note in his diary. His diary. That's it. If he has been round here and seen the file, he might have written about it in his diary. That's where he writes about everything else. I've got to go round to his flat.

I have keys to Julian's flat, of course. I take them with me but I only intend to use them if there's nobody to let me in. I ring the bell and wait. Winston opens the door. "I don't think Julian's back yet," he explains. "I haven't heard him come in."

"I'll pop up and have a look." I walk past him into the hall. "I can leave a note if he's not there."

Winston nods. "OK," he says and goes back to his room.

I set off quickly up to the attic but, at the top of the stairs, my feet slow down. What if Julian's there? What should I say? I go through the lines that I've rehearsed already in my mind. I don't knock on the door until I'm sure I've got them pat.

There's no answer. Everything is quiet. I put on my gloves before I try the handle. I'm being ultra careful now. He's left the flat unlocked. I walk inside. Everything looks normal except that I think he's left in a hurry. There are clothes out on the bed. He's taken off his best trousers and jacket and a smart clean shirt but he hasn't bothered to hang them up. He's just left them. I search through his jacket pockets and find the piece of card I gave him with my address. I tear it up and place the pieces inside my wallet. I wonder where he's left his diary. I don't think he'll have bothered hiding it. I find it inside a drawer.

I take out the diary and I know I won't have time to read it. I need just to thumb through the last few pages. I flick the diary open. Each page has different coloured ink, different styles of biro. Different types of memories. Even the handwriting changes. During the months I've been reading through it, I've been watching Julian grow up.

I find today's date: Friday, 28 March 1986, Good Friday.

The handwriting is scribbled, rushed, all over the place. When he wrote this he was upset. I read how the entry starts and the words hit me like a bombshell. I grip the table for support. I want to read on and finish but I know I haven't time. I have to hurry up and leave.

I don't have time to think and I don't have time to panic. I must take the diary with me. I have to get on with the job now. I can read the diary later. I take a deep breath. Is there anything else I have to do?

I look around the flat. I look at the posters on the walls and the shelves that Julian felt so proud of. I look at his books and clothes and the tiny kitchen with its poky stove and fridge. A long way from the kitchen in Windermere Road with its dishwasher and microwave. It must have been strange for him to give up all that. For a tiny moment I'm conscious only of the fact that I'm in Julian's room. I'm trespassing. Searching in secret corners, looking at private things. For the first time ever it occurs to me that I don't have any right to do that. I think of it as a desecration of another person's space, an act of exploitation. A rape of privacy.

I place the diary in my pocket then walk towards the door. I pause and look back. This is all I have of Julian. This room, this picture, this memory of what a room was like is all that I can take away with me. Except for the diary of course. I pat the diary, snug in my pocket like a baby joey. A being in its own right. *I'll play with you later*, I think.

I close the door behind me and walk quietly down the stairs. I don't want Winston to hear me. I don't want to have to talk to him again. I open the front door soundlessly. Before I leave, I look behind me. I look back at the dingy hallway and the stairs. This is the last time I shall see them.

I've parked my car a couple of streets away. I check that there's no one about. I close the front door quietly then I stride down the street and round the corner towards my car.

*　　　*　　　*

I cannot believe it. I just cannot believe it. I feel stunned. I feel as if a part of me has died. I've been round to Jamie's flat and I've seen his file, and my diaries, photocopies of my diaries, private things I've said, private thoughts that I never wanted anyone else to read. I can hardly believe it has happened. I just want to take myself back to three o'clock this afternoon and I want to erase the memory. I want to rip it out. I want it never to have happened. I don't want to see the desk and the file and myself, standing, staring, and the smell of burned cooking oil and smoke. It's like sitting somewhere homely and familiar and seeing part of the corpse of someone you know, its arms hanging out of the fridge. It's obscene. It's as if a part of me has died.

I keep trying to understand it all. Why should someone keep a file on me? At first I thought it must be a mistake. They'd got the wrong person. It was like a silly, bungling joke. There was someone else who had the same name as me, perhaps, and he was a Soviet spy and the Special Branch had mixed us up. But then, when I looked through the file, it really was about me: me going to a meeting, making a phone call; everything was true.

I circle round and round my room like a frightened gerbil. It's the way I trusted Jamie. That's what makes me so upset. If only I hadn't done that. If I'd just met him and thought there was something strange or something odd about him. Or even if I didn't like him. Then it wouldn't seem so bad. But the fact that I liked him and I trusted him. That's what I can't get over.

I think about when I went up to Jamie's in the lift. I remember feeling nervous, wondering whether it would be OK, wondering if he'd be pleased to see me or not. Then trying to reassure myself. Jamie's my friend, I kept saying. Of course he'll be pleased to see me. I have to trust in people's friendship.

When I knocked on the door and there was no answer

and when I saw the smoke, I was worried. I thought there might be something wrong. The flat could be on fire and Jamie might be inside, unconscious. I went inside to look for him.

It took a while for me to take things in because of all the smoke. There was a raw potato standing on the table. I remember that. A record was turning on the turntable but the pick-up wasn't down; and then when I walked over to the table . . .

I want to scream and run about. I feel as if I might explode. I've tried to pray, but somehow I can't concentrate. I can't seem to find God. I can't remember where I looked for him. There used to be a road, an avenue in my mind that led to God and now my brain is like a seething mass and I can't find the pathway to God any more. I want to cry.

I want to believe in God. I want to trust in people. I don't know who's involved in this. They could be anywhere. They could be anybody. They could be Rog and Cathy. They could be my parents. Some of them have to be somebody's parents. And do their children know? Who are they? These people. These spies. I don't know what to think.

I thought that Jamie loved me. I really thought he cared for me. I thought he would protect me, like the way he sorted out the policeman beating me up. Jamie was using me, exploiting me. I say the words to myself over and over because I know that I have to believe them. I can't. I just can't. I sit down and start to weep.

I decide to make myself a cup of tea. I have to pull myself together. I have to decide what to do. I put the kettle on, then I start walking round my room again. I make myself sit down. I stare at the carpet. Jamie has been here. He's sat down, there, on the floor. I can see the spot on the carpet where he sat. He's poured me drinks and played me tapes. The thought is obnoxious to me. What if he's been here on his own? What if he's been here when I've not been in? He must have. He must have been in my bedroom at home. He must have stolen the diary. I remember the night of the party. I remember talking to Jamie. I remember thinking how good it was to have a friend to talk to when Cathy was getting off with Andy. And all the time he was finding out about how our burglar alarm system worked. He must have taken the key out of my jacket pocket. Maybe he was wanting me to get drunk. So that he knew I wouldn't wake up. Maybe he was mixing my drinks on purpose . . . and when I was drunk he took my door key and the key to the alarm as well. I have a hazy memory; I remember staggering down the stairs and looking for my jacket. Only now I know why it was missing.

I go through the events, like a story, like a film I've seen on TV. Everything fits in place, but it only does so afterwards when the criminal has been arrested. And the thing I can't get over is that I'm the criminal, not Jamie. I laugh. As I make the tea, I laugh. Jamie has sneaked into my house at night. He's the burglar. He's done this to me. He's betrayed the trust I had in him. He's made me try to love him. He's left me feeling like a festering wound and I'm the criminal, not him. I'm the enemy of the state.

I sit down and drink the tea. I've started feeling frightened. What if Jamie comes round? If I don't turn up for the meal, then he'll come round to see if I'm all right. I know he will. I can't bear to see him. The thought of it makes me shudder. I don't feel safe any more.

I try to calm down. I can't think of anything to console myself. I feel betrayed. I trusted someone. I believed that Jamie cared for me. I cannot, just cannot face the thought that all the time he was using me. I feel violated. I thought there were things about me that he liked. I thought he enjoyed being with me. I thought that maybe something about me touched him . . . moved him . . . the way I felt so moved towards him. It makes me cringe to think about it. It makes me cringe to think I might have slept with him. And I was just a subject for his file. Someone, somewhere, paid Jamie for betraying me. I feel as if it's something I can't live with. I don't know how to live with myself any more. It makes me hate myself.

I have to get away. I can't face it. If Jamie comes round here, I know he'll tell me lies. He's told me lies all the time since I first met him. I'll want to believe him. I'll want to believe in all the lies he tells me because then that means that I don't have to accept what happened. It has happened. I can't cope with it; I can't live with it; I can't think of anything I can do. But I know it's happened and I can't escape from that.

I think I'll go to Astonbury. I think that's where it all begins, all the spying. I want to be there. I want to see it for myself. I won't be here then, when Jamie comes. He'll knock at the door and there won't be anyone to let him in. I don't know what I'll do after that. I don't think I can come back. I don't know how I can live with myself. I think I'll always be afraid.

LOCAL PEACE PROTESTER IN ACCIDENT RIDDLE

Enquiries have started taking place into the accident involving peace protester, Julian Christopher from Windermere Road in Bishopston who was injured last night by a police motor cycle escorting a cruise missile launcher from the US base at Astonbury.

The nineteen-year-old youth had been taking part in a Good Friday service organized jointly by the Christian Campaign for Nuclear Disarmament and the Radical Christian Fellowship. The peace protesters were standing outside the gates to the base when a convoy escorting a cruise-missile launcher emerged on a routine exercise through the Oxfordshire countryside.

Roger Brooks, also from the Radical Christian Fellowship described what happened: "When the gates opened and we saw the convoy coming out, some of us went to sit down in the the road. The police cleared us away but, as the motor cyclists approached, Jules appeared suddenly at the side of the road, rushed forward and sat down in front of them. There seemed to be no way the motor bike could stop. I can't understand why Julian didn't realize that."

Julian's parents live in the exclusive Windermere Road in Bishopston. His father, Joseph Christopher, is managing director of the DIY store, *The Joint.*

I don't know what to do.

I want to creep away, crawl away.

I feel like hanging myself.

I meant to get out of the job. I meant to tell the Boss. I meant to tell him that the organization was corrupt. It was nasty and evil and a waste of everybody's time. I didn't want any part in it. The only problem was that it paid me money.

I don't know what I'm supposed to do now. I suppose I have to sneak away. I've done the damage. Now I go back home, back home, back to HQ. I tell the Boss what I've done and he says, "Good boy. Good dog. Pat. Pat. That's another one less to worry about. Another subversive taken care of."

I start to clear up my flat. I don't have many things. A few books and clothes and records; I travel light. I have to because I'm always moving on. Staying out of trouble.

I go to the off-licence to collect some cardboard boxes. I have to clear out soon. People might get suspicious. People might start wondering: why did Julian go to Astonbury? Did he intend to harm himself? His parents might start asking questions. Somebody ought to ask some bloody questions. I need to get away.

Walking back to the flat with the boxes, I think about Julian coming round here yesterday. I think about how he said he trusted me. That touches me. I try not to think about it; I try to push the thoughts away. I can't crack up. I can't feel anything at all because I have to pack up and get myself away and I have to do that quickly. I don't know where I'm going yet.

I pack up the boxes as swiftly as I can. I pack my suitcases then I go outside and shove them in the car. I phone up the landlord and tell him I'll be leaving in four weeks' time. I have to give him four weeks' notice. The firm can pay the extra rent.

I take one last look at the flat. I'm not attached to it. I'll soon forget it. I just can't get rid of the picture of Julian coming here, standing here in the doorway, peering through the smoke, looking out for me. Someone he thought he could trust. Someone he wanted to love. Then seeing the file, seeing it spread out on the table, wandering over and having a look. I can't forgive myself for that.

I don't want to go and see the Boss. Not yet. I don't know what to say to him. I feel angry. It's all his fault. I was only doing my job. I was only doing what they told me, what they paid me to do. I've always prided myself on working hard, doing what I was told. Doing it well.

I drive out into the country. I don't know where I'm going. I park the car in a place with fields and sheep and outcrops of rock. It looks like the place Julian wrote about in his diary. I get out and start walking. I don't know where I am. The words of the song keep going over and over in my mind.

I can feel it coming in the air tonight
Oh Lord
And I've been waiting for this moment for all my life . . .

I don't know much about religion. I pretended to. I learned enough to get by. The way I had to learn about politics, about socialism and Trotsky. Just enough to pass unnoticed.

I don't know much about Jesus. I don't know whether he lived or not. I've never bothered finding out. All I know is that he was an enemy of the state. He was a real subversive. And whoever was the equivalent of Special Branch in his day–they were on to him in a flash.

Well, if you told me you were drowning
I would not lend a hand.
I've seen your face before, my friend,
But I don't know if you know who I am . . .

I remember reading about the way Julian felt when his

friend died. I wish now that I'd never invented my lover, Rob. I wanted to plant in Julian's mind the suggestion that he might be gay. I thought that would make it so much easier. Now I know what it's like to think that someone you care about might die, I wish I'd never done that. I feel as though I've committed a desecration.

When Rob died, Julian said he thought he'd gone to heaven. I've never believed in Heaven; I've never even thought about it. So I don't know where Julian would go to if he died.

I clamber up the hillside past the sheep and stand back and look at the view. It was somewhere like this that Julian came to pray. I've never been able to pray. I've never believed in anyone to pray to. I tried to believe in myself and I'm not sure I can do that any more.

Well, I was there and I saw what you did,
I saw it with my own two eyes.
So you can wipe off that grin
I know where you've been,
It's all been a pack of lies.

I look round at the villages and streams. I mustn't stay too long. I have to go away; but, first of all, I want to climb higher. I want to climb to the top of the rocks where I can look out right across the valley. Now I've come this far, I want to carry on. I want to go to the top.

I carry on clambering up the boulders. My feet aren't used to rocks and grass; they're used to driving a car. I still don't know what I'm doing here.

As I climb I catch glimpses of the road winding away below me. I won't be able to see it all until I reach the top. As I drag my feet up the last few hundred metres, I start thinking about my life, wondering where I can go next. I've always seen my life as a vertical progression, like a straight path. My dad was an officer in the army and he wanted me to go to public school and then to Sandhurst. I never thought to question it. I've always seen myself as getting on, working towards promotion, getting more responsibility, a bit more pay; clambering up to the top. Now I think I've reached a turning. Everything I've worked towards seems a waste of time. I wish I'd chosen a different job. I wish I'd had the courage to tell the Boss I didn't want the case. I wish I hadn't left the door open to my flat. I wish Julian wasn't hurt. I wish I could have my life again.

Panting, almost breathless, I reach the summit of the rock. I collapse and gasp the fresh air. The view is fantastic now. I can see for miles. I can see the roadway spiralling over to the hills far across the horizon. Sometimes it's hidden behind the trees; it disappears inside the tiny villages and then it re-emerges, travelling onwards like a stream.

I can feel it coming in the air tonight
Oh Lord

Maybe I've got too used to straight roads, travelling down the motorway, driving in straight lines. Maybe I ought to think in spirals, like a twisting staircase. Where you have to step backwards to move on.

When I was a kid I used to have a picture book called *Genesis*. It had bible stories in. The one I liked was about Jacob and his son, Joseph. The Jacob story had a picture of him dreaming. He dreamed of a ladder going up to Heaven with angels clambering up and down. The artist had drawn it like a stepladder, a kind of stairway up to Heaven.

I'd always had the idea there in the back of my mind that the staircase existed somewhere if only you knew where to find it. Like finding a pot of gold at the end of a rainbow. But maybe we have to build our own steps up, one at a time; we construct our own cages; we climb our own causeway; we build our own stairway to Heaven.

And I've been waiting for this moment for all my life . . .

The rock is hard and gritty. I fold up my jacket and sit on it. What I want is to move forward, to think of something constructive I can do. I'd like to find a way of undoing some of the damage.

Well, if you told me you were drowning
I would not lend a hand.
I've seen your face before, my friend,
But I don't know if you know who I am.

I stand up and pick up my jacket. I gaze around me one last time. I have to be moving on. I turn and start walking back down the rocks towards the grass and sheep. I think I'll drive straight to the ferry. I have my passport with me. If I can find a crossing tonight then I'll be in Europe by tomorrow. For the first time in my life I'll feel free.

I clamber down towards the grass and sheep. I don't know anything about God or Heaven and I don't know about spirits either but maybe there is something special that lives in people like Julian; maybe it rests in us all. But whenever we see it, it's on the side of those who are powerless and weak. The enemies of the state.

And, maybe, it's written down somewhere that for every time that a voice like Julian's speaks out for those who have no voice, then a guy like me has to come along and shut him up. Maybe Julian has to be a martyr; maybe someone has to destroy his innocence. I only wish to God it wasn't me.

I don't know why he had to have a father called Joseph who was a carpenter by trade. There must be thousands of people with those credentials. And they aren't all Jesus Christ. I only wish it hadn't all happened on Good Friday.

Well, I was there and I saw what you did,
I saw it with my own two eyes.
So you can wipe off that grin
I know where you've been,
It's all been a pack of lies.

Maybe if there is some goodness in the world, then it lives in people like him. I think I saw it shining from his eyes. He was totally innocent and unspoilt. I've destroyed that now. I've destroyed his trust in human nature. I've destroyed his innocence. I might have destroyed his faith in God. I hope not.

I look at the view for the last time then I turn and walk back to the car. I walk past the sheep and the rocks and clumps of gorse. I think of Julian coming here, or somewhere like it, and for a tiny second I can imagine his face and his smile. It's so real that I almost smile back at him.

Well, I remember, I remember,
Don't worry...

I have a strange feeling that Julian's not going to be easy to forget. I believe I'll think of him whenever I stand on a hillside and look out over a valley; I think I'll see his smile whenever I notice two people falling in love. I think I'll see it in the sunset at the end of a cloudless day. Like the words of the song he used to like so much: You can't kill the spirit; she is like a mountain, She goes on and on...

Jesus Christ, I loved him.